BEHIND
THE
SHADOWS

Horror Fiction by

RAY VAN HORN, JR.

Other Books
by Ray Van Horn, Jr.

Coming of Rage

Seven short stories reflect the human spirit and learning to rise up and meet adversity. To stand face-to-face with it, then overcome. Broken yet moving forward.

Revolution Calling

Two teenage boys navigate adolescence, maturity, and the highs and lows of life from the alienating stance of the heavy-metal subculture during the late '80s.

Testimonials

"Pick your shivers. Any shivers. Ghosts? Zombies? Things Unmentionable in daylight? Whatever your preferred chills, shivers, and icy winds down your spine, Ray Van Horn, Jr. has you dangerously uncovered and quaking in your armchair at a steady 150 mph… guaranteed to leave you both quaking, shaking and emphatically stirred."

–**Sheila Eggenberger,** author *Quantum Demonology*

"…A set of haunting tales… that grips you from the very first page – a masterful blend of suspense, raw emotion, and vivid detail. Stores that are atmospheric as they are unsettling, narratives to tense and evocate they linger long after the final story."

–**Joshua Viola**, *Denver Post* Bestselling Author, co-author *Legacy of Kain: Soul Reaver – The Dead Shall Rise,* editor *It Came From the Multiplex*

"Five Stars for Ray Van Horn, Jr… sure to captivate the attention of the horror community, who'll be chomping at the bit to read them all!"

–**Christopher D. Abbott,** author *Sherlock Holmes: The Watson Chronicles* and *Songs of the Osirian* series

"…An eclectic mixtape of Gen-X terrors, drawing from MTV videos, 80s horror flicks, EC Comics, late-night TV, Jolt Cola, Columbia House, *Fangoria,* Stephen King and *Hit Parader* magazine until the tape snaps and snarls up your boombox. He creates scenes with such clarity and vivid detail, you'll be asking yourself, 'Is it real, or is it RVH?'"

–**Jack Mangan,** The Heavy Metal Hall of Fame, Metal Asylum

BEHIND
THE
SHADOWS

Horror Fiction by

RAY VAN HORN, JR.

Raw Earth Ink

2024

First paperback edition November 2024

Cover art by Matt Slay

Library of Congress Control Number: 2024949652

ISBN 978-1-960991-42-3 (paperback)

Published by Raw Earth Ink
PO Box 2
Humboldt, IA 50548
www.raw-earth-ink.com

To all the long-established
and up-and-coming horror authors in the world.

We are a strange but proud breed.

scribimus indocti doctique poemata passim

Contents

The Darkest Side of Jericho

"How about doing something more productive than surfing your fantasy football picks and running a search for the bridge, Noah? Sync your iPhone up with Bluetooth, since you're better at that crap than I am."

Taylor eased off the accelerator of the Prius with a foot feeling antsier than usual. She smiled, glancing down at the black Vans Knu Skool loafer with its white laces and jagged wave design, both thicker than the shoe brand's Old Skool. Given to Taylor by her boyfriend of one year, three months, Noah, last week for her twenty-sixth birthday. Still tight, still in the process of being broken in. Being the same age as her, Noah had gone retro with his 1980s-styled black and white checkerboard patterned Vans. This despite Noah's frequent branding of Generation X as 'behind-the-times Atari fossils.'

"Sassy technotard," Noah goaded her from his side of the Prius. He had his thick fist wrapped tightly around the "Holy Shit Handle" above the cracked-open passenger window. The slight whip coming into the car licked Noah's muddy brown follicles off the char of his dense eyebrows. The breeze did nothing, however, to cool the sweat collected atop the tattoo of a spiky-toothed hellhound inked beneath his left ear. "The NFL draft party's tomorrow at Paul's. You've been quiet for most of the trip until now."

"The sooner the better, Noah," Taylor scoffed with a smirk indicating she was playing more than dictating. Unlike her beau, Taylor's slightly tanned neck was clear of any perspiration even with the window rolled up on her side and no air conditioning running. She'd braided her raven hair in accordance with this morning's forecast on her WBAX cell app announcing clear skies and a mild high of seventy-two degrees. "Paul can have you *and* those garlic wings I've got marinating for your stupid football thing tomorrow. Today you're mine, and I need that map now. I only have thirty-two miles to play with."

"I *told* you to fill up at the travel plaza before we got off 95, Taylor. It's not too late to swing back into Kingsville, you know."

"Bitch bitch bitch, always fill up at a quarter tank, so you've told me a hundred times," Taylor snickered back at him.

"It'll be another hundred before it sinks in," Noah sneered at her roguishly, the tinge in his voice indicating a welcome to the overt silence prevailing over their long drive from Gaithersburg.

"Now that's a low blow, damn. There's so much more to the Gunpowder Falls system than I remember."

"I could've told you that, Taylor. Been years since I've been out here hiking, but the place is massive."

"I forgot Jerusalem Mill Village even existed," Taylor said with a crinkle to her mouth matching the crinkle in her voice. "Half of Harford County must be packed into that wine festival back there. I'm halfway tempted to say let's ditch this chump change assignment and go get wrecked on some merlot, especially if Bordi is one of the featured vineyards. Hell, what they're paying me for this dumb haunted video journal would barely cover a round for each of us. Glad we hit the ATM before heading out."

"Geez," Noah cringed at his cell phone, pursing his lips for emphasis. "Post You's getting downright scary since it always seems to know where you're at. An announcement for the Jerusalem Mill Wine Festival just flashed across my scroller. It's running until 4 pm at the Grist Mill, which gives us a few hours to catch up to all the other lushes."

"Alright, Mr. App Happy, find me the Jericho Covered Bridge already."

"You sure you don't want to turn back for gas first? The Exxon's not far. I could use a piss, anyway."

Taylor flashed Noah a mock look of disgust, capping it with a spritz of amusement. She loved Noah for all his graces and even his occasional lacks thereof. He was smart, tech savvy, compassionate, and smooth in bed, even if he dressed like a schmo most days with his baggy jeans and oversized hoodies during the colder months. Today it was the baggy jeans and oversized *Ex Machina* t-shirt variety. As if Taylor herself had any room to condemn, cramming her broad hips into a pair of Noah's olive cargo shorts he never wore anymore, and strapping on a tank top spread with a fading print of the movie poster for *Paranormal Activity.*

Noah could irk the snot out of Taylor with his occasional wishy-washiness and dime-dropping mood swings. What Taylor loved most about him though, was his putting up with her admittedly sardonic ways, which she felt ready to spill over, the longer it took to find the Jericho Covered Bridge.

"The bridge isn't far away; I just know it. I want to get this video done and enjoy the rest of the day drowning in vino. Pee outside if there's a private spot to do it. Inside the bridge, if you're worried about being seen, as you usually are."

"That's rude even for you, Taylor," Noah snapped in a way he knew would bring him accusations of being oversensitive. "You may be a bigger tyrant than Heather Donahue in *The Blair Witch Project.*"

"At least I don't have a dirty behind," Taylor cracked in homage of one of the found-footage horror classic's more memorable jibes.

"Well, this website I just kicked up for Jerusalem Mill says Jericho Bridge is somewhere 'adjacent' to the village. Seriously, I'm surprised we have decent Wi-Fi out here in the boonies."

Noah's coasting through the application buttons on Taylor's console inside her Prius was so fast she had no time to see the menu windows vanish from Liquid Metal on Sirius XM, which was playing a tasty grinder from Cannibal Corpse at a hideously low volume, over her Bluetooth link. Noah was so rapid, the Prius announced its synchronization to his iPhone quicker and louder than George "Corpsegrinder" Fisher, ralphing his death metal measures at a criminal muffle before vanishing altogether once switched to Bluetooth mode. Onscreen, a map of the area skittered and scrambled into place, locking onto their position.

"Anytime now, Babs," Taylor muttered with an upward blast from her lips.

"*Follow the highlighted route,*" spoke the robotic female voice of Babs, Taylor's name for the car's babbling, cackly GPS system computer speak.

"Babs probably thinks you're as much of a tyrant as I do."

"That just guaranteed you a trip to the couch tonight. Or worse, your place, alone."

"Hello, sweaty palm, my old friend," Noah larked with a spritz of mock annoyance. With the slower posted speeds and less of a draft intake, he nudged his window down further with his right forefinger before snatching the Holy

Shit Handle again. "It's eight-tenths of a mile after we turn from Glenbauer Road. Before then, you're looking for—"

"In two-tenths of a mile, turn right onto Jerusalem Road."

"Beaten out by a femme bot," Noah grunted.

"Which you once told me sounded kinda sexy. Of course, this comes from the same guy who dishes on *A Quiet Place* but wanks all over the *Pacific Rim* sequel. A masterpiece, I believe you called *Uprising*, boo? As if, Kaiju Stan."

"Stan kaiju, totes," Noah said with a flush to his cheeks.

"Turn right onto Jerusalem Road."

The lush May greenery grew denser as Taylor picked up the pace, pushing the Prius up to forty miles per hour, then forty-five in their approach of Little Gunpowder Falls. Scatters of dead leaves and branches from the prior fall and winter seasons were painstakingly pushed to the sides of the road, leaving to wonder who exercised cleanup detail around here, the park service or Mother Nature herself.

"Jesus!" Taylor exclaimed, stamping down on the brake pedal as a squirrel jumped from roadside and halted its fuzzy-tailed tracks smack in the road.

"Glad there's no traffic behind us, shit!" Noah grumbled, clutching his guts. "Aaaaand my bladder's not gonna hold over that. Pull over and lemme out!"

"There's no shoulder *to* pull over, Noah!" Taylor shrieked, spanking her steering wheel horn. The squirrel's eyes shot so wide in recognition of the sudden threat to its life, it scampered off to the other side of Jerusalem Road before vanishing into a pile of thickets leading to the woods beyond. "Piss like your life depends on it! Knowing how long it takes you to whiz, I'd better throw on my hazard lights. Twenty-six is too young for a prostate exam, Noah, just saying."

"Yeah, yeah, adulting sucks," Noah muttered as Taylor pushed the button to her blinking yellow hazards, the metronome *click-click-click* sounding ominous amid the relative seclusion. "You worry about the road. You know I freeze up if I feel like I'm being watched."

"Sounds like an ongoing *you* problem that's becoming a *me* problem."

"Ehh, shaddup."

Fortunately, no vehicles came from either direction as Noah completed his task into a freshly sprouted eddy of crab grass skirting the barely visible white line marking the scant pavement between road and vegetation.

"Not that I'm complaining," Noah mumbled, tugging on his fly as he plopped into the passenger seat. He'd been in such a hurry he'd forgotten to zip up. "I'm shocked there's been no traffic so far. Makes me wonder if the legends behind the bridge scare people off."

"We'll find out soon enough," Taylor said, throwing the shift into drive and taking off quicker than necessary. Her rear tires gave a remote squelch in rapid succession, prompting faint laughter between them both.

"*In a quarter mile, turn right onto Jericho Road,*" Babs chirped through the car's speakers.

Finally, the first sign of life, as Taylor slowed in mid-turn onto said road with Babs' continued prompting.

A cherry red Chevy Silverado pickup blocked their way momentarily from its tight-swung turn off Jericho Road, aiming in the direction Taylor and Noah had just come. The bulk of the truck and the driver's unaffected cutoff was so much, Taylor had to brake hard again to avoid being clipped. A man nearly as wide as the entire left side of the truck's cab snickered in derision at them from behind his half-cracked window. An NRA sticker showing a Glock amidst a shot-out target and the slogan GROUP THERAPY was planted on the rear driver side window of his Silverado.

"Rude, fat hick!" Taylor hissed, leering venomously from her side of the Prius. "Make America Gluttonous Again!"

"Good one," Noah said, tossing a middle finger toward the rear of the car, knowing the gesture was futile, much less undetected.

"This shit isn't worth the twenty-five bucks," Taylor grumbled. "My deductible is $500 if Jabba the Gun would've tagged us, even if it would've technically been his fault."

"Then why bother? This would be, what, your sixth video now? Those cheap asses at Haunted Hellscapes Maryland are just going to doctor your footage with CGI 'shadows' and planted 'voices' over your monologues like they did the other clips. Only you and I know we've found diddly squat in our purported ghost hunts. We do nothing remotely considered FOMO and you know it. The only thing faker than Haunted Hellscapes is my ex, Hannah."

"And she's ancient history," Taylor said to Noah with a warning tone reflective of her annoyance with the Silverado driver. "At least she'd better be."

"Chill, already, wow. There it is. Welcome to the border between Harford and Baltimore Counties and our mystical destination of the week."

Babs confirmed it with, *"You have arrived at your destination."*

Ahead of them, decked in reddish heavy timber, was the eighty-eight-foot-long, fifteen-foot-wide arch-trussed Jericho Covered Bridge. Under the summertime glare, it looked like an earthbound, wooden portal to the underworld.

Taylor slowed her approach, not because of any precaution for oncoming cars from the opposite direction, but because of her awe of the curved timber trusses inside the bridge, including the suggestive engulfment inside.

"Man, they still make paint schemes this intense?" Noah quipped, pushing his face as close to the windshield as he could without smearing his forehead against it. "This is some sinister-looking shit at first glance."

"The longtime myths of flower girl ghosts, burnt old women and demonic monkey-things sold the assignment."

"Don't forget the rumors of dead folks swinging from the rafters."

"My parents used to take me out to all these covered bridges up in Lancaster, Bird-in-Hand, and Intercourse, Pennsylvania," Taylor whispered, letting the Prius idle at a faint hum before the engine fan kicked on with a tick and a whirr, adding a baleful ambience to the scene. "Amish turf, where horse-drawn buggies use them more than us English outsiders. Lots of red on those bridges, but nothing like this one. This is like a structure oozing blood. Take some pictures, Noah."

"Sure," he complied, scrolling and tapping his cell phone with his thumb even quicker than he'd navigated the in-car computer before frowning. "Getting a lot of glare through the windshield."

"Here, allow *me,* nerd," Taylor egged him, opening the passenger window from her side of the car.

"As I said: tyrant," Noah teased back, undoing his seat belt, then arching his waist through the open space from the car and snapping off a few shots of the bridge. Settled back into the seat, he swiped through a quick succession of three clear shots, showing them to Taylor, who gave him a silent nod of approval.

"Jericho Covered Bridge was built during the Civil War for wagons and carriages and this one's been renovated three times since," Taylor blurted, already in commentary mode without a camera inducing her. "I've seen many covered bridges decked in red two-by-four wood, but never anything this — "

"Vivid."

"Vivid," she repeated. "Spot-on."

"Terrifying, if you let the area folklore get to you."

"Hundred percent."

Intertwined undergrowth belched from beneath the wood-staked girders curving into the opening of the bridge, indicating the local park service may have kept the incoming roads cleared, but they wanted nothing to do with the main attraction itself.

"Well, I'm down to twenty-nine miles before I need gas," Taylor heaved with excitement. "So let's do this."

"I don't see a turnout on this side to park on," Noah said, betraying a hint of concern to his voice. "Maybe on the other?"

"In my experience, it's about fifty-fifty having serviceable places to park at covered bridges."

"Nobody's coming, Taylor. I say go for it."

"Let me know if you spot any simian sentinels blocking the way. Ohh-wee-oh, wee ohhh-ohhhh."

"Makes me wonder who started such all these ridiculous legends."

"People more bored and boring than us, babe," Taylor said, nudging the car window controls with her two left fingers, raising them back shut.

Taylor began her approach into the covered bridge, taking it at an easy five miles an hour.

"So far, a lot of bunk," Noah mocked as the sunlight disappeared and they entered the obscure shade inside the bowels of the bridge. "Though I'd be lying if I said I wasn't getting a little weirded out right now."

"As long as we don't stall out," Taylor said with a dry smirk. "A common report I found online is people's engines dying momentarily at the center of this bridge."

"Good thing you opted for the fluid flushes with the oil change last week," Noah said sardonically. "Though I'm telling you right now; I see a handprint on any of the windows, I'm dumping you in the back seat and driving us out of here faster than—"

"Whoa!" Taylor gasped, once more stopping the car on a snap, exactly at the middle section of the bridge. Even with their windows closed, the aroma of musk, of *fugue* was apparent.

"What?" Noah nearly shrieked. "What? Oh, Christ, don't tell me the car just—"

"Gotcha," Taylor gibed with a wrinkled wink and playful pat on Noah's inner thigh before she burst out laughing.

"You witch," Noah snarled in a pout, pulling his leg away from her in protest. "Get us through, already."

"Oh, get over yourself," Taylor returned in as gentle a pitch as she could muster, but still rolling her eyes. "There's nothing to the myths here. Let's find somewhere to park on the other side, shoot the clip, and call it a damn day. I want wine more than I want a ghost to show up, at this point."

"We gotta go back through the bridge, you know," Noah said, shooting his girlfriend a sarcastic look she missed altogether from the near darkness inside the bridge.

BUMP-BUMP-BA-DA-BUMP BUMP-BA DA-BUMP-SHUNK! the bridge beneath them went as the Prius scooched along the steel girders. A final KA-THUNK! emanated as they cleared the other end of the bridge.

"I see somewhere to park," Taylor said, matter-of-factly as she spotted Noah inhale and wipe his left cheek before dabbing newly collected sweat from his forehead. "Slim, but enough for someone to get by, if needed. Hopefully we can knock this video out in ten minutes or less."

"I didn't like how that felt in there."

"Is it your first time inside a covered bridge?"

"Yeah."

"All this time we've been together, I've never taken you for claustrophobic."

"I'm not, but something's way off here. It's like—"

"Take it easy, will you, Noah?" Taylor snapped, the agitation in her voice rising. "We won't be long, okay? I'm sure our luck with no traffic will run out soon, so let's make this a hit and run, then roll out."

"We're going back inside on foot?"

"Well, duh, Noah," Taylor taunted him. "What's with you? You didn't act this way at Point Lookout, Glenn Dale Hospital, or St. Paul's Cemetery. In fact, I recall it was you who'd said, quote verbatim, 'The Fletchertown Road Goat Man is a bunch of bullshit.' Why in the world are you so upset out here?"

"Forget it," Noah sulked. "I'm not going to explain myself, but I've got a feeling this is a big mistake."

"I didn't drive an hour-and-a-half just for a joy ride, Noah! An unexpected side diversion into some house red wine, okay, cool, but if you think Heather Donahue was a camera hogging autocrat, I'll be blunter. Man the hell up and get ready to shoot."

"Asshole, is what you are."

"Look, I'll make it up to you in the village, Noah," Taylor sighed. "I paid my credit card down last night, so all rounds are on me, okay? Get your phone out and start rolling. I'll do a historical briefing as we approach the bridge."

With a grimace, Noah pointed his cell phone at Taylor while punting a loose rock on the road.

"Rolling," he mustered, looking past his girlfriend, as if expecting something worse than a car to come crashing out of the bridge.

"So, we're here on the outskirts of Kingsville, Maryland," Taylor spoke, getting into narration mode.

"One of the prettier destinations we've been to for this series. Behind me is the notorious Jericho Covered Bridge traversing Little Gunpowder Falls. Locals have claimed for decades this thing is haunted. Easy to say when there are so few covered bridges left in America, much less Maryland, as they have the lion's share of them all over Dutch Country, Pennsylvania.

"My boyfriend, Noah, and I have just gone through the bridge by car, and so far, we've seen nothing. Jericho Covered Bridge was built after the Civil War in 1865 and it was listed on the National Register of Historic Places in 1978. That was the year my mom was born, funny enough. Her generation and those older than her, attest to a lot of spirits and mythical demons guarding Jericho Covered Bridge.

"Which is not to say someone in their mid-twenties like us is averse to believing in ghosts and the supernatural. It's why we keep doing these videos for Haunted Hellscapes Maryland."

"You're blathering," Noah interjected in a snide tone.

"Cut!" Taylor hissed back at him, making an angry slashing gesture across her throat. "What the fuck, Noah? You shoot, I do the talking! That's how it works! I did a thing and got my Bachelor's in Mass Communications. *You* went to Lincoln Tech for —"

"Oh, sure, sweet humblebrag, Taylor!" Noah shot back at her. "Total douchery."

Taylor stopped and realized her mouth was still hanging open until she closed it long enough to swab at the corner of her right eye which was filling up with tears.

"I don't give a shit about the winery anymore," she whispered. "I just want to get this done, get some gas, and drop you off at your place. I'm so done with this."

"Look, Taylor—" Noah said with a sigh before realizing he'd left the video running on his phone, even if it was pointed down toward the road.

"Point and shoot," Taylor instructed him with a severe look upon her face, which vanished as soon as he complied.

"I—" he attempted to say, but Taylor cut him off by resuming her commentary.

"I read a few testimonials recently from high school students at Patterson Mill who make the same claim of sightings as their parents and grandparents did of a young female ghost carrying flowers over Jericho Covered Bridge. Apparently, the girl has been known to shriek soundlessly at those who catch her, which would be wild to see if it was real."

As Taylor backpedaled toward the entrance of the bridge, she paused and felt a powerful lift of her hair at her neckline from a sudden breeze. It came from behind, splaying her hair atop her head, as if pushed from a gale force.

"Oh, my God, tell me you got that!" Taylor squealed at Noah, in half terror, half glee, hurriedly getting back into gear. "It's a peaceful May afternoon, no wind whatsoever today. No threat of rain or storms in the forecast. In fact, Noah and I *were* planning on hitting the wine festival we spotted in Jerusalem Village after this, but I'm telling you, though, this place is at a quiet standstill and *that* just happened. My hair! Wow!"

"Taylor, honestly," Noah said with a rising urgency. "It's total coincidence."

"No, *no!*" Taylor retorted with her own potency. "Something happened! You can't tell me it was just a fluke! Noah, this is a chance to do something real! Screw you, Haunted Hellscapes Maryland; keep your goddamn twenty-five bucks! I'm going full viral with this. Come on, Noah, follow me!"

"Taylor—"

"Come on!" she snapped.

Knowing she was dead serious, Noah pursued with such pinpointed, head-weaving caution that he managed to avoid stumbling on a divot in the road leading into the covered bridge.

"Of all the urban legends surrounding Jericho Covered Bridge," Taylor began again, "its most unsettling claim to fame is the numerous reported findings of apparitions hanging from the rafters of the bridge. Some say these are the ghosts of former Civil War soldiers having taken their own lives inside the bridge. Others say the suicides were local teenagers who were so deeply in love and couldn't be together, they went all Romeo and Juliet style and hung themselves from high up. Still others claim the spirits are lynched runaway slaves from a darker time in American history."

It was Noah, not Taylor, who'd suddenly screamed at the manifestation hovering at her right shoulder. It was the body first, then the scarred face of an elderly woman wearing a transparent, if threadbare shawl over her slumped and saggy shoulders. A face charred, hideous and so full of rage it seemed ready to gnaw into Taylor.

"What?!?" Taylor bellowed, more out of anger than fear, considering Noah's exclamation had rattled her. Also considering she had no idea what was lurking behind her.

"Stop, Taylor!" Noah shouted, starting to back away. "Get out of there now and don't look back!"

"What, Noah? What? If you're trying to hit me with some kind of get back, I—"

"No, dammit, I can show you! The camera got it all! The burned old lady, she's real! I'm telling you, Taylor! Real! She was about to nail you!"

Immediately, Taylor whirled around, gaping into the depths of the covered bridge.

"Where? There's nothing in here, you idiot!"

"I'm telling you, get out *now!!!*"

"Oh, shut up already, Noah! Here I thought we had something this time!"

"Christ, Taylor, there she is now!!!"

The cell phone hit the metallic roadway inside the bridge, capturing an image of the rafters, accompanied by shared offscreen screaming.

From the YouTube streaming show, *Mr. Macabre*, Episode 74:

Rounding out our top five creepy video picks for this week and sitting in pole position for the creepiest I've ever aired, comes this submission from Richie C. in Havre de Grace, Maryland.

I don't know how you fake something like this, but as always, you be the judge.

A ghost-chasing couple from Maryland went to a covered bridge outside the town of Kingsville, reported for generations to be haunted. The bridge sits at the meeting point of two counties and was built sometime after the Civil War ended. Local legends have sightings of a ghostly little girl who carries flowers to an old crone who was burned so badly area historiographers cannot identify her.

You can do more research online about the Jericho Covered Bridge near Jerusalem Mill, Maryland, but the thing which scares me, your indomitable host, Mr. Macabre, is the ongoing reports of visions of hanging corpses inside the bridge.

I say this as a set-up for what you are about to see. My personal opinion? So much happens in this video to discount it altogether and it is the most realistic, frightening thing I've ever seen. No empty hyping, viewers, it's that scary. I have sped up the timing toward the end as there is a near two-hour lag from the couple's screams and a lingering shot of the covered bridge's rafters until you see —

Well, like I said, you the be the judge. Drop me your thoughts in the comments section. If you haven't already subscribed to the Mr. Macabre channel, do so first and be sure to smash that like button! This video may be forcibly removed by YouTube soon.

A video spool of monologue from a twenty-six-year-old woman named Taylor Brisbon is interrupted by a blast of air against her back, lifting her hair up. A menacing synthesizer streams in accompaniment.

"*Oh, my God, tell me you got that!*" Taylor shrieks giddily. "*It's a calm May afternoon, no wind whatsoever today. No threat of rain or storms in the forecast. In fact, Noah and I were planning on hitting the wine festival in Jerusalem Village we spotted after this. I'm telling you, though, this place is at a quiet standstill and that just happened. My hair! Wow!*"

"*Taylor, honestly,*" her companion named Noah Riem, groans off-frame, as the ethereal music dubbed into the clip, drowns him in a discordant dirge.

In less than a minute, Noah is freaking out as his cell phone camera captures what appears to be traces of a snarling, seared old woman behind Taylor. The apparition's blackened, sinewy mouth is protruding like she's about to chomp on the oblivious Taylor.

Pandemonium ensues as Noah can hardly keep the camera steady. Mr. Macabre has placed a punctuating synth strike designed to heighten the jolt of the scene. It's as if Noah's drunk and staggering backwards from the entrance of the covered bridge. He's backing away and imploring Taylor to come with him immediately.

The camera swishes back and forth, barely capturing the hasty fright of Taylor, who appears to be wrestling with herself. If she can see what's attacking her, she doesn't show it. What she does show is outright terror, belting out screeches worthy of Janet Leigh, the godmother of scream queens.

Taylor succumbs to subjugation upon the metallic supported throughway inside the bridge. The action is so swift, it's not wholly decipherable what's dragging Taylor down. Yet something is, for sure, blurry as it may be.

Noah's screams join hers, as the camera abruptly flips in midair, the image twirling helter-skelter like a bungee plunge gone horribly wrong.

The synthesizer calms, leaving a lurid ambience as the clatter of the cell phone striking the bridge gives all the shivery haunt needed. Left in its wake, is a visual of Jericho Covered Bridge's rafters with faint peeks of sun, dust motes and a swooping bird dashing across the screen.

A jiggly, rapid fast forward of the video moves the image beyond its sustained nothingness until it resumes in real time. Still nothing.

Nothing.

A cheesy hammer strike of synthesizer greets the audience along with the precipitous ghastly image of Noah and Taylor hanging from the top of the bridge, their necks twisted, eyeballs protruding, expressions of shock and anguish. Their deaths appear fresh, even with the garish palettes of purple and gray flushed across their twisted rictuses.

From the online comments section at *Mr. Macabre,* Episode 74:

WANNABEDED666: "Fake!!!"

GloomGurl94: "Best video shown here, but yeah, fake. Nicely done, though, guys."

SATANSPLAYMAYTE: "If it *is* real, I'm booking a flight into Maryland right now, 4REALZ!"

WANNABEDED666: "Nah, total CGI. The ghost woman's a joke! The hanging part was rad, though. Hey, Dead Meat, give these guys a Golden Chainsaw Award or something! @SATANSPLAYMAYTE if you wanna be *my* playmate, reroute your flight to Indiana."

SATANSPLAYMAYTE: "F.U. @WANNABEDED666"

WANNABEDED666: "Kinda the point. LMAO!"

MissFit 38: "How do you explain the hair blasting part? You can't tell me that was a rig. Scary AF.

WANNABEDED666: "Filmora and AI copilot editing works wonders. I call squad goals."

On May 25th, 2024, a 2019 Prius registered to one Taylor Brisbon was located near Jericho Covered Bridge and impounded by the Harford County Sheriff's Office. No one came to claim the automobile.

Taylor and her boyfriend, Noah Riem, were never seen again.

The Carnelian Pick

"Alright, Seth, you flew halfway across the country for this. Get to the point."

The sound of ice cubes clinking about a highball glass with the fused stencil "1961 VINTAGE: AGED TO PERFECTION" around one-half of the cylinder dished the only noise inside the study at a critical point in this meeting. A reunion, under better circumstances.

It was, for the moment, quiet enough to detect a drifting thump of bodhran, tabor and timpani, accompanied by bagpipes and double reed shawm through the netting of the screened window in Roderick's office. A frolicky resonance from the Maryland Renaissance Festival, whooping it up in its third weekend of eight a mere two miles away. Far flung, besotted cheers of *"Huzzah!"* rang from Flemish, Victorian, and Celtic-garbed cosplayers during the hardy game of Olde English make believe in a clarion-filled party zone called Revel Grove.

Paradoxical to the friction inside the estate bearing the supercilious namesake of its owner, Slade Town.

The opponents, former spandex-clad hairballs, living a rock 'n roll spectacle of their own making and demise, Pryme Kutz. Lead vocalist Roderick Slade and his longtime holstered guitar sidearm, Seth Fitzpatrick. *Billboard* victors and heavy metal outlaws of a rock hard, ride free era of the Big Eighties belonging to neither of them anymore.

"Just my being here should make the point, thief," Seth said with impudence while beholding the glitz around him, mounted gold and platinum record sales awards he was plenty familiar with. Mock 33 1/3 vinyl never seeing the caress of a stylus, planted to the walls in Roderick's office. A leveler must've been used since the perpendicularity was absolute.

"What, you lose your copies?" Roderick blurted haughtily, like he had entitlement beyond master of the 12,000 square foot Tudor-styled stone and thatched manor outside of Crownsville. "Did you hock them for blow or something? The way you keep looking at mine like you have a—"

"First off," Seth fumed, thrusting his highball glass forward in condemnation at Roderick like most accusatory people would do with their forefinger. "I've been clean eleven years, screw you, and my awards are stashed inside a plastic tub in my walk-in closet. I have far less real estate to hang them, than this palace you've surrounded yourself. Shame you never found someone to share it with, Citizen Kane. Candy sends her regards, for what it's worth."

"She always *was* a sweet girl," Roderick said in monotone, dialing things back a notch, though pouncing on the opportunity for an additional potshot. "Only woman I know who stands by her man tougher than Tammy Wynette."

"That's a sketchy indictment coming from a crook. Like I'd ever hit her, you bastard."

"Hmmph," Roderick said, taking a pull on his own glass of bourbon, sans ice, his furtive grin assuming all the coolness his drink needed. All a front. In truth, Roderick felt disconcerted, the same way he'd felt the last time he was in Seth's presence. Fauld's Theater in Knoxville,

Tennessee, a dubious distinction, not just for housing the final stage Pryme Kutz played on together.

"I wish this overdue visit was about putting the band back together for a summer cash grab, but you don't need the money, obviously. I appreciate the drink, but let's cut the crap, Rod. You know why I'm here, so just give it to me before the local Rennies clog up 97, alright? My flight back to Kansas City's in less than four hours and BWI has been enough of a bitch today."

To look at the two adversaries, ex-bandmates, with a neutral eye, they were nowhere near their peak. Their graying, gnarled hair (Roderick's being snagged into a tight ponytail like the elder version of Terry Silver transitioned from *Karate Kid III* to *Cobra Kai*) were flaccid, pale shades of the outrageous plumes they'd aerosol-caged with Aqua Net decades ago.

A matching set of pooched bellies betrayed years of excess having caught up to both men who used to show off their cut abs from low-cut elastane slings. Instead of the ball-crushing striped Lycra pants casing their bulges, each man now wore one size up saggy jeans. No doubt their long-ago fans would call the sad recession in their senior years cringeworthy.

"I'd be doing you a favor by saying I got rid of it," Roderick said, hiding a sudden bluster in his voice easy to match the agitation diffused across his visage.

"Yet you know I'd call bullshit on you without a second thought."

"Look, Seth, no matter how far you've traveled, I didn't invite you here. You really should go back home to your world-famous barbecue and Swope Park and forget this sentimental campaign of yours. I know what you're after, and I was hoping all these years of silence meant you'd come to see it for the evil thing it is. I'm not giving it up, though, and that's me trying to be your friend."

"My *friend?*" Seth exclaimed in outrage. "My friend was Roderick Slade, a guy who used to pound a fifth with me backstage and quote Plato and Descartes in the same breath as Howlin' Mad and B.A. Baracus from *The A-Team.* He would say 'I love it when a plan comes together,' and we all took it like our own rally charge."

A faint but traceable smirk leaked across Roderick's face, wiped away as soon he became cognizant of it.

"My friend Roderick Slade used to challenge me to endurance eats at Waffle House," Seth rolled on, jerking his eyebrows upwards with further reflection. "Roderick Slade, a guy who gave his band buddies packs of tube socks as gag gifts before each tour. Where the fuck did that guy go?"

"The bunk socks, heh, good times," Roderick deflected with a bigger grin he let stay a moment longer before adding, "but the third person speak is Jeff Bridges all the wrong way."

Seth paused a moment to pull from his iced-down bourbon, letting his lips quiver from the initial sting and bared his tobacco-stained teeth. More scoff than recoil.

"Roderick Slade, the same guy who cannibalized my riffs to a greenhorn producer and a hack session guitarist for a solo record any novice could've done better with Pro Tools — along with something *else* he pocketed. The guitar pick was given to me, not you, Rod, and I want it back. Now."

Roderick thought about the fictile, carnelian-colored guitar pick which had summoned Seth to his home from a ludicrous distance. He knew why Seth wanted it. He also knew why he had to keep it *away* from Seth.

Seth swished the cubes within his thinned-down bourbon, calculating his gyrations as if to impose maximum annoyance upon Roderick with the tubular clinking. "Top shelf poteen here, *friend.*"

"Much better neat," Roderick countered, maintaining the chit-chat portion of the engagement out of caution more than amenity, since things had taken the expected downward spiral. "Single barrel rye heavy mash batch, 46.5 volume, master craft out of Bardstown, Kentucky. $230 a bottle. You can taste the oak when you don't water it down. Don't expect a refill, Mr. Clean."

"Candy gave me a compelling reason to stick to booze only these days," Seth returned, rebuilding his own snidery as he shook his glass again. He tossed his eyebrows upwards once more, this time as a snarky provocation. "A single of expensive bourbon for a guitar pick pinched by a sneakthief, though — hardly a fair exchange."

"Seth, it's a shame all around what happened to Pryme Kutz, but why, after *twenty years* since we — "

"Laid the band to rest at the end of an abbreviated touring cycle for a tanked album which should've been left inside the soundboards," Seth finished for him, jerking an even louder retort from the ice cubes, since he'd managed to cajole irritation upon his host's face. The small triumphs were often as sweet as the endgame. *"Cold Revenge* was karmic by title alone. First album the pick didn't bring us the same mojo as its predecessors."

"Could be because you'd turned into a vicious asshole because of the damned thing, just saying."

Now it was Roderick's turn to play poke-the-bear. He flashed *his* teeth, opaquer than Seth's, seizing upon the opening he'd made.

"Like hell," Seth whispered, reeling from the accusation.

"Seth Fitzpatrick, golden god of the frets. Yeah, we made millions once that Polish kid in Poznan traded picks with you. I mean, what were you even thinking, man? I admit it, we all got better as a band because of your newfound 'talent.' It was cheating, but it was also glorious.

Look where it led, though. That orange-swirled guitar pick changed you in other ways. I can see it in your eyes right now, Seth, the same appetite for destruction from an old man's eyes. You want the pick so bad I can feel it radiating off you."

"You're outta your—"

"You remember that time at the Poughkeepsie Ramada Inn?" Rod blurted, cutting Seth off with a lofty oscillation of his head. "You threw the television at Lee after he tried to snatch the pick while you two were horsing around. Lee said your cussing tirade was worse than a Marine and an Army grunt in a pissing match, and the glare in your eyes, Seth—Jesus, I won't ever forget it. I came in at the tail end of that shit show. Hell, the entire third floor of the hotel heard you threatening to slit our throats if we ever tried getting the pick from you again."

"I-I don't—" Seth stammered, his eyes darting around their sockets with anxiety. They scurried from Roderick to the mounted records to everything else he could survey in the study, including a cherry oak executive desk to his right and a bookcase in a shadowed corner with leather spines and titles in copper colored embossment. He was too out of sorts to read the book headings, even if that hopeless anecdote was the least of his worries right now.

All Seth knew with assurance was Roderick had the carnelian pick. He just *knew* it.

"It happened," Roderick said as if it were indisputable truth.

With a wilt he hated himself for, Seth yielded. "I don't remember that at all."

"I also take it you don't remember losing your shit when the pick split the strings over and over on your Gibson Sunburst?" Roderick pushed on, already done with his drink and placing his glass on his desk, the desk's length nearly stretching the cold distance between them.

"After enough busted strings from your insane playing, you smashed the Sunburst right in the middle of a take for "Love Oracle." Of all songs, a goddamn power ballad! Then you reamed us all out, like it was *our* fault! We were holding you back, you said. Then you had the absolute balls to demand an extra ten percent cut, just because you'd made the covers of *Hit Parader, Circus,* and *Rip!* You fucking prima donna."

Again, Seth looked stupefied, struggling in all earnest to find any validation to Roderick's condemnations. Thinking about the two-and-half hour flight, versus twenty-six hours driving to Crownsville, Maryland, Seth hadn't expected any of this refutation. He came on a mission and the mission was faltering.

"You were trying to turn Pryme Kutz into motherfucking Slayer with your preposterous thrash lines, Seth! You'd shred over-the-top midtempo rhythms with that pick unless we reined you in. If anyone can understand, it's me, but you were so afraid of losing the pick, you'd stash it under a pillow every night."

"I don't remember that either," Seth said, sucking all the air he could fill his lungs with. He slurped his bourbon the same way a child would a plate of sauce-sloppy spaghetti. Seth darted his tongue out the side of his mouth to catch the residue spewing from the left crease.

At the same time, desperation was begging entry into the most abstract place inside his brain.

That, and a new, unseen voice, sounding like it had slid close to Seth to serve him a wet willie inside his right ear, before scaring the living shit out him.

Kill him for it if you have to…

"What the hell—" Seth gasped at an unseen voice so musky and ribald it could've been Barry White out of his love unlimited grave. In this case, more of a rapist than seduction artist, from the afterlife.

If Roderick heard it, he made no indication.

Finish your drink, smash the glass over the filching prick's head and cut his throat with one of the shards. He stole me from you. Your guitar parts too, the dirty fucker. Payback's a bitch, though, right? You said that sooooo many times the last time we were together. Knoxville, Tennessee, that's where it happened. The end of the road, the day I went missing.

If Roderick had heard Seth's mumbling or detected the sudden spark of terror sending a jolt down the wrist holding his drink—his playing hand—Rod showed no sign of any of it. He was pushing his own agenda.

"Trust me, pal, I talk to Lee on a semi-regular basis. The TV incident came up in our last conversation. He's still bitter and doesn't send his hellos, though he says he and his old lady Tisha, are doing fine. They own an occult shop somewhere on the outskirts of Salem. Considering Lee wrote "Love Oracle," the whole endeavor in the mystic arts makes sense. Gary, *ehhhh*—Lee said he's on this fourth stint in rehab after his current band, Other Than the Knife, dumped him. Fucking bassists."

We're magic together, Seth, the voice needled, barging past Seth's shattered cerebral shield. Seth wanted to scream, but somehow, he knew better not to. *Let's kick up that mojo again, whattya say?*

"So, w-where's it at?" Seth stuttered, openly revealing the first sign of his mounting breakdown. The sweat pooling at his forehead had less to do with the alcohol scrubbing his bloodstream. Fear was doing a far rowdier job.

"It's telling you right now to do me in, isn't it?" Rod sighed, pursing his lips.

Don't listen to him, the deep baritone influence nudged at Seth. *Don't you miss how it felt, people cheering for you, the photographers in the pit focusing more on you than the rest of the band? It was* you, *man. Well, you and* me, *of course.*

"I don't have to hear it speak to know the pick is talking to you, Seth."

"What?" Seth squeaked, the same way he did as a thirteen-year-old getting cracked across the face by his mother having caught him with a dime bag in his bedroom. With a wobbly hand, Seth set his highball glass down on Roderick's desk. He was suddenly no steadier than an elderly barfly on his fifth round. "How could you…"

"All cards on the table," Roderick interrupted with dominance without raising his pitch. "I know the pick better than you ever did. It chooses when it wants to talk, and it's had me, not you, all these years. It's been thankfully quiet until now, but somehow, it's made a connection with you, and fuck a duck, like we used to say in better days, here you are at my door. Yeah, Seth, I stole the pick. I also stole your parts. The riffs only, not the arpeggios, scales, whammy chords, and all that wanking crap you got from the magical pick. Hell, I should never have done it, especially giving it to—"

"McGee," Seth whispered, flash-checking the framed sales distinctions, proof of arresting days filled with laser effects, pyro charges and echoing bombast having left Seth with permanent tinnitus. A life nevertheless worth living. One he wanted for a return engagement; tinnitus be damned.

That amateur, Jack McGee, the undetected voice snorted. It snorted—if a demoniac, or whatever the freaky baritone phantom was—could do such a thing. Bad enough it could *talk,* for Christ's sake. *He couldn't play with his dick any better than he did me. Come on, Seth, I've been waiting all this time. Kill Rod. Do it this very minute. He won't tell you where I am, but you'll figure it out. Do it. Open him up and let the crimson flow. Only then can we resume what we started together, into glory ride.*

"Jack McGee," Seth repeated aloud as the bantering inside his head jacked its incessant chucks at him. Seth's hurrying heartbeat reminded himself of the pulsing intro to Pryme Kutz's whumping party anthem, "Past Midnight."

Do it! the supernatural intonation pestered.

"Jack McGee, yeah," Roderick confirmed with a nod and a momentary shutting of his eyes before adding, "He wasn't you, not by a longshot, even with a cheat."

No shit, jerkoff!

The assertion inside Seth's ears was so palpable it became lunacy, being unable to see what was projecting it. If only Barry White had lived long enough to take a walk on the wild side of metal like unexpected seniors Pat Boone and aristocrat of the Nosferatu, Christopher Lee.

"Seth, listen to me, man. Drop this nostalgia shit and go, before something terrible happens. You get that pick back, I promise you'll regret it."

He's the only thing stopping you from making millions, just like the old days, Seth! You don't need this feeb who can't hit the side of his house with a stray acorn than a falsetto anymore. You sure as hell don't need no puny 850 square foot bungalow in the Midwest. Damn, how the mighty have fallen. It's pathetic, my man. Pathetic.

"All I can do is apologize," Roderick said, glancing toward a wooden lock box on his desk the same width and size of a cigar container. Cedar with a rust-tinted lock and no key to be found inside its eye. "Seth, this shit I pulled wasn't worth losing a friend over, I admit it. I'm sorry, okay? Hell, the only way anyone can get a hold of my solo album, *Stray Fading,* is on Spotify! I tanked on my own! I got what I deserved, including years of guilt and bad advice from a cursed piece of plastic I've had to keep hidden all this time. Biggest mistake of my life, to be honest."

"Coming off your tongue, Rod, the word 'friend' sounds toxic," Seth snarled, balling his fists again, disregarding everything Roderick said beyond that.

That's right, tell his ass off, then kill him.

"Don't you see what's happening here, Seth? It did the same thing to me all those years ago in Knoxville. That's when I nicked it. It told me then it wanted *me*, not you, even though I couldn't play guitar for squat. I was dumb enough to fall for the pick's ruse, and every day I sound more ridiculous saying it."

Claim what's always been yours, Seth. He deserves to die.

"I can see it's doing the same thing to you it did after Poznan," Roderick droned with a rolling up of his eyes then dropping a giveaway glance toward the cedar box on his desk. "That Polish con artist knew damn well what he had, and he wanted rid of it. He screwed us all."

"Maybe," Seth relented, only a smidge. "But I was meant for that pick. I let it go, even though I've always suspected it was you who took it."

"Funny enough, Seth, I made my fortune after the band was done, but not in music. I control more than a third of total shares in one of the biggest international coffee exporters out of Brazil. Did having a dark enchanted pick help my portfolio? I suppose so, but what that damn guitar pick had me do after I recorded *Stray Fading* is what I'm ashamed of the most."

"What do you mean?" Seth quipped, taking a step backwards instead of forward.

Don't be such a pussy, the burly voice nagged at him, seeking a trigger point to reignite Seth past the clouds of doubt closing in on him.

"Seth, that thing's an instrument of chaos. It *gets off* on chaos. I didn't kill you for the damn pick like it wanted me to do back then. Keep that in mind before you go off the deep end, alright? I took it after our big, dumb fight in

Knoxville sent us all home sulking like a bunch of limp dicks. It didn't like Jack McGee using it any more than me, but he laid down the tracks for *Stray Fading* in three days and then he rolled out, grateful for the below-scale pay I gave him. Some guys are just that hard up and shame on me for exploiting him. I figured the pick would mesh with McGee, but no, the guy wouldn't even be able to fill a hat playing outside one of the honkytonks on Beale Street using it. I figured I'd never hear from the guy again, but a month after *Stray Fading* was mastered, Jack called to tell me his playing wrist was all screwed up and he hadn't gigged since recording with me. You see where I'm going with this?"

"You're blaming the pick? Come on, Rod."

"That same voice you're hearing? Like Isaac Hayes carrying a mean streak, ordering you to do something I know you're not capable of? Seth, it *laughed* at me after I got the call from Jack. He got carpal tunnel a month after the sessions, and you know what else?"

"Enlighten me," Seth responded, squinting at Roderick with a suspicion he knew was wrong, also knowing the pick meant more to him than any grisly truths affiliated with it.

"Jack heard the voice too, though not quite as often since it rejected him. Jack told me he'd heard *'You peel a wet fart with more conviction. Do the world a favor and kill yourself.'* The poor schmuck told me this when he came around again to my place, insisting I pay for his medical bills. His description of the voice was to the tee, and it creeped me the hell out. Seth, I'm telling you this in the hopes you'll be on your way to BWI before I finish. The pick, the goddamned *pick* — it told me to send Jack away and to blackmail him with video I had running during the recording sessions. I thought I'd shut it off for the day, but the camera caught Jack snorting coke off the bare ass of someone who was not his wife. Underaged chick, too. Game over for that guy. I told Jack to piss off before I turned him in. When's the last time you heard from or about Jack McGee?"

"I don't know, Christ," Seth grumbled irritably. Even with Rod's shameful admission of his guilt, all Seth wanted was his carnelian guitar pick back.

Wait for it, the unseen speaker egged at Seth, finishing with a sinister rumble-laugh.

"Jack hung himself in his basement the day after he came to see me. I tried burning the pick after that, but the thing's impervious. I've tried throwing it out several times. It's always made its way back to me. On the doormat, in my mailbox, on top of the microwave. Inside my goddamn box of Wheaties, of all things! I'm telling you, Seth, leave now, before something awful happens. Let me make this right somehow and save your damn life."

You wanna be the best guitarist on the planet again? the voice pounded at Seth, as if sensing it might be snuffed amidst the battle of wills between two men who knew it so well. *Then do it. Kill him! Do it. Do it!!!*

The sag to Seth's eyes set a stony milieu which Roderick picked up instantly. His appeal to his old bandmate had fallen flat. The sudden spring inside of Seth's pupils then told Roderick he was about to lose much more than the appeal.

"No, man, don't do it!" Roderick screeched, knowing this was the end of the argument. The end of his life, even. "Don't listen to it! It'll destroy you!"

"If you say so," Seth said, far more collected than he was moments ago. The murderous blaze to his bellicose stare spoke of something far more insidious. "But the pick is mine, and as you know, I have a plane to catch soon."

The cedar box on Roderick's desk was a blur between both men. Seth seized it with hurried, lethal intent. Cattle at a slaughterhouse had more time to react to the slug of a metal bolt into their brains. The crunch of the box splintering Roderick's skull would've been sickening to hear if anyone were to bear witness to Seth bringing it down with all the force he had inside his sixty-three years of life. Briefly one of the most prominent guitarists in the world.

Now perverted into a courier of death.

With the office window open, Seth could hear the echo bombs of whumping drums from the Renaissance Festival, followed by distant-thrown, tandem hails of *"Huzzah!"* Merrymakers and fantasists caught in the moment of praising cavalier reenactors busting lances inside a simulated jousting arena.

To Seth, the accolades sounded cast to and only for him.

Up went the box again and down it came overtop Roderick's dome, already stained by his own blood between the graying fibers. Roderick's ponytail jiggled instead of snapped in reaction to the second hit, which made Seth even curiouser. He paused as his former friend swooned, his eyeballs rolling upwards like they wanted out of this life before their carrier.

"Huzzah!!!"

"On the mike, at center stage," Seth crooned deliriously, caught inside a transfixed moment from the past in a sold-out arena in Boston, Liverpool, hell, Poznan, Poland, where the whole fucked-up thing with the carnelian pick started. "Roooooooderick Slaaaaaaade!"

Seth turned the still-locked cedar box inside his hands, checking to see if it had split anywhere. Seeing a fragmented corner of the box with blood and a few strands of Roderick's snagged hair, Seth grit his teeth, his eyes twin incarnates of madness as he screamed, "Wait'll you see the curtain call, baby!"

Instead of hoisting it up and down again, Seth switched his posture, remembering how natural a whiffleball stance used to come to him in his teens. It felt the same nearly fifty years later. Huzzah, indeed.

Seth knew as soon as he had the cedar box busted open, he'd be rejoined with the pick. He even had an idea for a new band name after being two decades out of the scene. It would be legendary. Once again.

Everything flew after Seth squared up and swung for the fences: the lid to the box, splinters of wood, blood, one of Roderick's teeth. The carnelian pick, though — nowhere to found amidst the carnage.

"Huzzahhhhh!"

"Son of bitch," Seth growled over Roderick's moaning, which sounded more like sobbing. His vengeance-fused eyes scuttled all around the office floor amidst the broken pieces of the cedar box, the pooling blood around Roderick's bashed up head and broken shards of glass. Seth had been so quick, yet so blind in his violence he hadn't seen, much less felt, both highball glasses blasted upon the floor.

"Nice fake out, fooling me with the box, Rod. Now where the fuck is it?"

Before he slipped into unconsciousness at Seth's feet, a faint chuckle glided out of Rod's bloodied lips.

You're going to have to dig deep to find me, the arcane voice not belonging to Roderick pressed into Seth's eardrums, full of repetitive squishiness from his drubbing pulse. *I'm sure you can dig up a carving knife somewhere in this fortress. One of those glass pieces might do, but it'll be longer and messier that way. Might make us late for our flight.*

"You've gotta be kidding me," Seth groaned, his stare compelled in the direction of Roderick's swollen abdomen.

ᴛᴛᴛ

Less than a year later, a retro rock band calling themselves Infinity Kings released their debut album, *Life's Been a Circus*. Infinity Kings amassed mostly positive reviews, hitting a mean average of eight out of ten on many critics' scales, a perfect five for five at a few commercial music websites. The album charted slowly the first month of its release, hitting 121 on Billboard before the breakout single, "Rapid Fire," stormed up the singles chart.

Infinity Kings became as much a talk of the wilting rock scene as youngblood revisionists, Greta Van Fleet. A reviewer for Temple of Rawk called *Life's Been a Circus* and Infinity Kings; "a much-needed shot of adrenaline to a languishing rock state."

Four of Infinity Kings' bouncy band members were no older than twenty-five. It was sixty-three-year-old Seth Fitzpatrick, former guitarist of Pryme Kutz, who gained the most notoriety with a new lease on life. The kids kept up with his precipitous shredding to later score the band Rock Album of the Year and Best Newcomer honors. Earning the affectionate nickname "Pops" from his junior bandmates and their coming-of-age demographic, Seth took Best Guitarist Award from *Guitar World* magazine and, even as a western Yankee, was recipient of the SEGA European Guitar Award. The tag *Comeback King* followed Seth everywhere.

Seth was never seen with any guitar pick other than the same carnelian strumming piece and the industry marveled how effective it was on both the up and down strokes. It became a hot topic in the band's interviews, since press photos for Pryme Kutz showed the same pick lodged beneath the strings on the neck of Seth's now-favorite Ibanez. Seth never once mentioned where he'd gotten the pick, still impossibly smooth around the edges after decades of in-and-out playing. He simply called it his "go-to."

On the fifth date of a ten-day winter leg through Germany, Czechoslovakia, Hungary, Romania, Bulgaria, Albania, and Poland, Infinity Kings' touring bus crashed on the icy outskirts of Zerkow, near its neighboring city of Poznan. All on board survived, save for Seth Fitzpatrick and his wife, Candace, who had been touring with the band.

Infinity Kings' rhythm guitarist, Zack Starr, losing a mentor in the accident, spotted something on the side of the road while waiting for Polish first responders to arrive on the scene. Awash with grief by the unfathomable loss, Zach was nonetheless drawn to an object twenty feet away from the crash site.

It practically called out to him with his bandmates, roadies, tour manager, and bus driver locked in shellshocked embraces. It was the creamiest shade of orange splashed with vanilla swirls running around both sides of the triangular plastic piece, one Zach recognized as well as anyone in the band, but none had ever been so close to. Until now.

He would've wanted you to have it.

Death of the "S"

November 27, 1992.
An east coast American comic book shop.
"Sheeeeeeezus…"

Not even the buzzsaw guitars of Jim Martin, the pulverizing snare smashes of Mike Bordin and the caterwauled mantra of *"Surrrrpriiiise!!! You're dead!!!"* from Faith No More's Mike Patton could overpower the screechy slashes of the wilting wiper blades across Dennis' windshield. The rubber was beginning to trail at the lower end of the right blade, wriggling with each groaning pass. Dennis likened it to an electrocuted worm, swearing to replace it once he got paid the following week. This every other week payday shit made the simplest things harder than they needed to be.

"It's not over yet," Dennis croaked along with Patton, already feeling routed before his shift began in a half hour. Black Friday. No classes today. Only a paper due in Causes of the Civil War the following week, which he had originally slated to knock out this afternoon. Dennis had planned on typing up the paper and later screwing off with a *Twilight Zone* marathon he'd pre-recorded on the family VCR.

A perfectly plotted day off.

Foiled by the Death of Superman.

Dennis inched his Dodge Colt hatchback through the Cranbrook Shopping Center parking lot. Black Friday: most people were expected to clog the malls, not an independent comic book shop catering to a core demographic of man-boy geeks. A "boutique" comic book shop, as Dennis' neurotic, three-months-divorced boss, Stu Rapaport, branded it. "Dweeb Central," Dennis had heard not one, but three, people call it.

Yet here they were, and where they'd been in the aftermath of the Death of Superman. Everyone and their mothers popping into the store all week asking for it. The first printing had sold out in less than an hour on day one. People you never usually saw in a comic shop showing up in droves: bankers, doctors, jocks, local senators from both sides of the political fence, gangstas in their oversized flannel shirts and do-rags, police officers still wearing their uniforms and squawking walkie-talkies.

Girls.

Dweeb Central had become less of a retail store and more of a wake, with a line of customers drifting all the way to Fremont Food. It was such that the store's chubby female manager-on-duty, in her red smock and retro beehive hairdo, was waving her arms frantically at the queue pushing into the corrals of her store's dwindling carts. As if by doing so could magically whisk them gone.

Likewise, the other end of the shopping center was slammed. Mattress Mania was having a 30%-off sale, while its profitable chain neighbor, Harriet's Fabrics, was cleaning up with their storewide buy-one-get-one deal. The lady bargain hunters ravaging Harriet's Fabrics, regardless of shapes, sizes, and fitness, all looked ready to throw down on each other — over *textiles*, of all things. Textiles imported from China and Vietnam amidst a soaring sense of nationalism, sparking all true patriots to buy their goods stringently marked with a *MADE IN THE USA* label.

The myriads of people in line at Gary's Comics emanated their own exasperation. Many had huddled in close quarters against the frosty elements, having arrived hours ahead of the store's opening time of 10 am.

Some were staging a morning party amidst the raw drizzle, bringing with them bags of Hostess donuts or rolls of bagels with jellies and cream cheeses along with thermoses of coffee and hot chocolate. A maudlin tailgate to an unpleasant, fictitious event robbing The Last Son of Krypton of his proverbial life in defense of a proverbial America.

Not since the lines for *The Empire Strikes Back* and *Return of the Jedi* - both cinematic events finding people turned away or standing hours for their chance at a later showing - had Dennis seen a queue so daunting. People camped out for those movies back then, just like some folks still did at department stores hosting TicketMaster for U2, Michael Jackson, or Prince concerts. Dennis cringed to think what time the people at the head of the row had arrived.

"Come on, guys, they're *second printings*," Dennis fumed as he scanned the crowd. All in prolonged wait for a reprint copy of DC Comics' gangbusters second volume 75th issue of Superman titled *Doomsday!*

Even Burger King, plotted in the center of the strip mall, had all they could handle with customers squashed inside plus the bumper-to-bumper cars clogging the drive-through. It was apparent many of those tramping in and out of the "Home of the Whopper" in their sopping winter gear, were doing so merely to take advantage of its restrooms. A good handful were finger-pointed by the recognizable "S" insignias peeking from their unzipped coats, denoting Superman's family crest of El across their chests. Dennis already knew they'd be coming his way in the store soon: wet, shaggy and potentially ponging of spoiled Prell, Herbal Essence, and Head and Shoulders.

The death of Superman had been covered on the major networks, *Newsweek,* and *Time*, as if a real-time hero had put his or her life on the line for the salvation of mankind. For weeks, the *Doomsday* slugfest came out through four different Superman titles, tied in with *Justice League of America* #69. The latter of which, no comic retailer in the country, much less Gary's Comics, had; due to an apparently sparse print run.

The alien murder machine dubbed Doomsday was a failed genetic experiment from prehistoric Krypton, flushed hyperspace into a metallic holding cell deep beneath the Earth. Silly enough of a premise, Doomsday's skeletal protrusions emaciating from his jawline, limbs, shoulders, and, worst of all, his fists, achieved the unthinkable. Doomsday's bones were so sharp he was able to gouge the Man of Steel's chin and puncture his ribs before the final round taking both interplanetary adversaries' lives.

The double death-punch at the end of *Superman* #75 was heard around the comic book world, presuming one had the imaginative power to put sound to graphic art. Dennis likened it to battleship cannonade, not that he'd ever been on one. It seemed to fit the blaring BDAMMM! BRAKAMMM! and KRAKATOOM! onomatopoeia blasting throughout the Doomsday epic. Bombastic visual sound effects even non-comic book fans couldn't help but put mouth to letters in goofball mimicry. The same way screeching horns accompanied each cartoonish BIFF! POW! and ZOWIE! placard dashed across the fight scenes in the old *Batman* TV show from 1966.

Stu had offered a pre-payment package for the entire seven-issue storyline carrying over the character's multiple titles, and his ploy had worked. Readers and investors alike had plunked down their deposits, guaranteeing them the whole story, including the fan-described "death issue," which had rocketed in sales as the hottest comic book of the year. Perhaps ever.

The looks of dejection on those who'd missed out was downright pathetic in Dennis' mind.

"He'll be back, losers, mark my words," Dennis growled inside the car, drifting his Colt into a spot far from his usual across the store entrance. This time all the way down near Mattress Mania. The windshield wipers grunted louder now that the post-Thanksgiving sprinkle was calming down. Mike Patton continued his yowling through the frenzied slam his band supplied for him. Patton peeled off the exact pitch of outrage Dennis imagined Clark Kent himself bellowed in his final throes with his Superduds shredded down to his bare pecs. As Dan Jurgens and Brett Breeding imagined him, Superman had a rug pillow torso for the aggrieved Lois Lane to bawl into.

Out of his car and threading his way past the many cheesed-off women at Harriet's Fabrics, the sudden squelch in Dennis' guts nearly released something worse once he was shouted at by someone at the head of the line in front of Gary's Comics. It was a fatso father wrapped in a navy-blue pea coat with his arm slung around his fatso son, clad in an oversized sweatshirt with, no guesses needed, a crackled iron-on print of Superman's trademark crest.

"Line cutter!" Fatso Father roared.

"Yeah, get outta here, jerk!" trumpeted a petite woman behind them. Bantam she may have been, her mouth made up for her slightness. She wore a black fleece pullover looking as raggedy as the rest of her. It gorged upon her small frame, dangling past her knees. Dennis couldn't help but think of it as a motley outfit some of the Goth chicks he knew back in high school would've worn with their shocked Siouxie Sioux spreads and blanched skin like Dream's antiutopian (if kinda hot for a drawing) sister Death from *The Sandman* comics.

Dennis might've chuckled at the comparison, if this raggedy girl hadn't made him angry along with Fatso Father. He wished Raggedy Goth was more reticent and introspective like Death as she continued to sound off at him.

"We got here at 6 am, kid! You don't just roll up all high and mighty like you're better than us! If you're lucky, they ordered enough this time, but get in the back where you belong!"

"I *work* here," Dennis sneered, doing little to erase his defiance as he rapped on the locked glass door with its **CLOSED** sign facing him.

"I know your boss," Fatso Father said with the self-entitled airs of a professional kvetch. "Gary has a first print waiting for me at the counter, *cover price*. The bagged version nobody else in town has for less than a hundred dollars. Harold Hemlich, I used to go to school with Gary."

Dennis knew bullshit when he heard it. The guy might as well go balls-out and claim to have an original copy of Superman's first appearance from 1938, *Action Comics* #1. Dennis couldn't resist throwing some fine-tuned shade back at Fatso Father.

"Sir, not to contradict, but Gary Rapaport died in '89, before my time here. Before then, he'd passed the store on to his son, Stu. We have a polybag first print of seventy-five, true, but it's first come, first serve to whomever pays the mark-up price of $150."

"That's criminal!" Fatso Father harrumphed as his porker kid wriggled his left forefinger into his ear and dug inside the canal. The kid's eyes ballooned like he'd gone plumb crazy trying to scoop an intruding gnat out, if it were still gnat season. "Who in their right mind would pay $150 for some outlandish *comic book?"*

"You'd be surprised, sir," Dennis replied, wiping away the satisfied smirk from his face as quickly as it had manifested. He heard a set of keys jangling from the other side of the glass door.

"You're late," his boss grumbled as he inched the door just wide enough for Dennis to squeeze through without sending unintentional signals to the antsy throng.

"Sorry, Stu," Dennis said, quelling an urge to yell.

"Hey, man, can you put one aside for me?" hollered a bearded fanboy six people deep wearing an olive-colored thermal top and a black snow hat with the white spider insignia once belonging to Peter Parker, now to his vengeful nemesis, Venom. The guy had his forefinger tucked into a partly shut hardcover compilation collecting Bronze Age stories of *The Mighty Thor* circa the 1970s.

"Yeah, me too!" someone else shouted behind him. He was half-lunky and half-bulbous, his swollen arms belching from the hiked sleeves of a Flash tee. His engorged belly, spawned by a presumed diet of beer and junk food, strained the bottom jags of the Fastest Man Alive's lightning bolt avatar. The doofus had no coat on and the incredulity to whine, "We've been out here shivering in this stupid rain just to get one! I'm gonna be majorly pissed if you guys sell out again!"

The door whisked shut behind Dennis with the familiar *snap-clunk* of the lock being reset.

"I wanted you here an *hour* early to help count inventory, Dennis," Stu admonished him. "It's Black Friday, in case that little tidbit eluded you. Where's your armband?"

Dennis wanted to say, seeing it bounce back and forth between the opening of his leather bomber jacket, *Bad enough having to wear ties and button-down dress shirts in a nerd oasis to peddle comic books, but ripping open three polybag copies of the most profitable comic book in history, just to fish out the memorial armbands and make us wear them like actual interments?*

"I'm still a half hour early," Dennis said instead, rubbing his stomach, while glancing down at the Fred Flintstone imprint on his tie. Fred was peeling off one of his trademark censures of his wife, Wilma, with a detonative word balloon containing her name projected overhead. Dennis then plunged his hand into his jeans pocket, jerking out the black remembrance prop in question with its oozy, garish red 'S' logo blazed on it. "Armband, check."

Outside, Fatso Father was cupping his eyes and pressing them against the front door for a looksee inside.

"Harold Hemlich?" Stu grunted. "I haven't seen that pompous puffball in here since Dad was about to pass me the reins. I never forget a face. If that's Hemlich's chunk-a-butt kid, the apple didn't even get far away from the tree's roots. The schmuck once tried to pawn us repro DiMaggio and Mantle cards. I can still hear Dad bawling him out, 'We don't sell sports cards, but even if we did, you can't expect us to be so lax at our jobs we can't detect fakes.' Pure Rapaport gold right there."

"He claims to be a friend of Mr. Rapaport and entitled to a discount on an original 75."

"He *would,* the cheap slug. Harold Hemlich can have one of these second printings at cover price like everyone else," Stu said indifferently. "He's as offensive as his name."

Dennis swooped his gaze upwards at the ceiling and the imposingly huge comic book and sci-fi memorabilia hanging there, none of it for sale. An entire suspended microcosm where The U.S.S. Enterprise and a *Star Wars* Tie-Fighter crossed into a parallel universe. Pitted against swooping Green Lantern, Wonder Woman, and Captain America statues ten times the size of the action figures available for sale in the store. A huge stuffed Bugs Bunny held sentry in the deepest corner of the store, lifting a carrot twice the size and length of anything found in the produce department at Fremont Foods. No doubt wanting to call everyone below a "maroon" if he was capable of it.

"So, Dennis, how much cranberry sauce did you put away yesterday?"

This came from Chet Dellone, by nametag the store's Assistant Manager, though by work delegation, no more elevated than Dennis except when Stu left the store on lunch break.

Chet wore a ratty, dark tie over a yellow Arrow button down already betraying sweat stains beneath his armpits. The same executive shirt brand as Stu's, only Stu was carrying a sky-blue palette around his shoulder-slumped frame. Chet's pitch-black necktie had nothing to do with manufactured grief for Superman laying it all down in the heat of battle. It was the only tie Chet owned. Wrapped around his clammy right arm was one of the gimmick mourning armbands Stu had ordered his staff to wear today.

Chet stuck his hand out to Dennis for a sociable slap in passing.

"Enough to send me down the Hershey Highway this morning," Dennis said back with a bare chuckle, keeping his voice low as they scooched toward the rear of the store out of Stu's vicinity. Stu was brushing dust off a table set up toward the front of the store with his palm, swiping the residue down the side of his gray slacks to erase the evidence. He was oblivious to his clerks.

"Sorry I asked," Chet cracked with a smile while leaning in toward Dennis. "Stu's being more of a douche than usual. I don't think he spent Thanksgiving with anyone yesterday. You know his kids aren't speaking to him; they've sided with their mother. Stu was planning a microwaved Swanson turkey dinner alone and I doubt he even did that much. Between you and me, I don't think he ordered enough copies to get through today. If there really was such thing as a Spidey sense, it'd be raging all over my dome."

"They're *second printings*, Jesus," Dennis bristled. "If this had been the death of Wolverine, Rogue, or Storm, this whole thing would be a spaz insurrection only. Those we're used to."

"Most of those clowns out there don't know the X-Men, dude," Chet said, giving a partial shrug. "Superman, everyone knows. You'd think Christopher Reeve himself died. Sidebar, Wolverine will never die. He can't with his auto healing factor."

"Chet, you'll lead that spaz insurrection well before Professor X," Dennis replied with a dramatic eye-roll. "Secret for your ears only, I opened a temporary pull box down at Phantom Zones to get the whole Doomsday run. It sucks for Stu with the divorce thing, but his 'customers first' policy is bullshit."

"Traitor," Chet chortled with a belly laugh bouncing his tie off his noticeable pooch.

"Why should I have gaps in my collection because of these investor pricks? I *read* my comics, point and endpoint."

"Did they get you *JLA* 69 as well over there? Not even Stu's magic has been able to—"

"*Of course,*" Dennis interjected, trying to keep his voice down as Stu looked downright panicked as the clock inched toward 9:40. "For all my griping, the Doomsday story was worth the cloak and dagger. If for nothing else, to see Guy Gardner's face beaten to a pulp."

"I read it, Dennis, and you're disturbing."

"Someone hadda smack Guy Gardner around. His hair stylist should be next."

"If Stu finds out you crossed company lines—"

"Meh, he won't. He's been so absorbed with how the Death of Superman affects his profit margin to pay *me* any attention. For example, I was supposed to be off today before this all-hands-on-deck crap. I still have my paper on John Breckenridge due next week."

"Better you than me, pal. Maybe we'll sell these reprints out fast and Stu will let *me* leave early."

"Like you have anything better to do on a Friday other than DM campaigns for bigger dorks than our usual clientele. You down with RPG? Yeah, you know me!"

"Dick," Chet scoffed with a chuckle.

"I'm not the one who likes to spank it to a *Dragonlance* module."

"Actually, I'm going to *make* it with my elf ranger archer, Albina, after we finish running through *Dragon Dawn*."

"And your dorkette's non-gaming name is?"

"Albina, like I said," Chet fired back with a wink. "Get a double of tequila in her, she palms a D20 better than anyone I've ever seen. Fantasy fighting's in the lower spectrum of her many talents."

"Do you make her roll for initiative first?" Dennis cracked, making a shafting gesture with his fist, carrying with it more lurid insinuations than a die cast.

"Punching in now, instead of at door open would be appreciated, Dennis," Stu called out in such a smart tone it made Dennis cringe. "I ordered 300 copies flat, but I think Leaf Distributors shtupped me. One of these cases feels awful light, and if these books all fly out of here in a hurry, Lord help us. It'll be Supergeddon Part Two."

This unexpected gibe made Dennis laugh. Chet settled for a dry smirk as he spot-checked the racks to make sure the comics were aligned alphabetically and by sequential issue number. As a rule, Stu only kept the two most recent issues of a comic series on the main wall. Those would be later rotated out and filed to the back issue drawers, marked up by a dollar (or two, depending on the popularity of the title), sheathed with a protective plastic cover and backing board.

At the new release shelf, an entire tier had been cleared for the *Superman* #75 reprints with two identical, tacked pieces of cardboard decreeing the edict in magic marker: LIMIT ONE PER CUSTOMER.

After clocking in, Dennis slid his Superman tribute armband up his left arm overtop the long sleeve white Van Huesen dress shirt his father had given him straight out of his closet once Dennis started the job. He felt and heard the cheap felt of the armband begin to split at the bottom, right beneath the 'S.'

"Cheap shit," Dennis muttered, shuffling out of the stock room. By ritual with every shift, Dennis tapped the chiseled hip of ex-KGB turned Avenger, Black Widow, clad inside her gray bodysuit with his two right fingers. Drawn, inked, and colored with such spandex-snug idealism, she might as well have been nude. The poster depicted Natalia Romanova in her close-cropped ginger hair, ready for fisticuffs with a cocked gloved fist and a badass spider avatar planted over her left breast. The print was tacked to the back of the stock room door like a secretive centerfold. "Hero porn," the scene pervs called it.

Back on the floor, Stu shoved a pile of Superman comics at Dennis to take over to the new release shelf. Though the first run of *Superman* #75 had come and gone a little more than a week ago, the purple scoring which overlaid the swooped white lettering of the comic book's title (versus blue over yellow on the original printing) and the denoted

Roman numeral II punctuated next to the copy price of $1.25 classified it as a new release.

Stu's eyes were bugging and glazed, his cheeks flushed with manifest anxiety, as if the store were opening in the very next minute.

"That's twenty-four copies. Make two sections of twelve."

"These'll be off the shelf in nanoseconds, Stu. If people don't slit each other's throats for the copies on the front table."

"Your job is to direct any stragglers to the extras on the shelf," Stu told Dennis without acknowledging his concerns. "If we can get through this with any sense of efficacy, it'll be worth opening the extra hour for Black Friday this year."

Outside, someone had slipped around to the front door, thumping, not knocking on the glass through his gloved knuckles. He was half the size of Harold Hemlich but roughly the same height as Harold's teeth-chattering kid.

"Come on, guys, it's freezing out here!" Stu, Dennis, and Chet could hear muffled through the glass.

Stu gave no verbal response, only a castigating, repeated tap upon his Donald Duck watch, which pointed to 9:47. If one were to look closely at the watch, one could see Stu appeared as miffed as Donald himself, personifying the flustered *POP!* word balloon over the incensed duck's snarling bill.

The interjector disappeared as fast as he'd arrived, shamed back to wherever he'd slipped out of line. The lead catcaller was, of course, Harold Hemlich's cocky offspring. Those in the little rabble-rouser's midst picked up his loud, squeaky chant in tandem, "BACK OF THE LINE! BACK OF THE LINE!"

It grew loud enough to be mutiny.

"Wow," Chet muttered at the scene as the mob swung up another ruthless mantra, "NO CUTBACKS! NO CUTBACKS!"

"They weren't this unsparing for the *first* printing," Stu said, his eyes widening then sagging as he turned his back to an even louder cheer. One would have to assume the crowd had chased the target of their wrath gone altogether.

"In high school, I used to smuggle comic books inside folders to trade with my buddies so I didn't get beat up," Dennis carped.

"Take that case and give me a count when you're done," Stu ordered Dennis after the first task had been completed. "Chet, we'll do the same protocol as first printing day. You'll do crowd control. Dennis will work the floor. I'll take register. *One* copy per customer. I'm not concerned about leftovers, because we won't have any. Unlike those dead weight *Alien 3* trading cards I'm still kicking myself over."

"Got it, Stu," Chet said, flashing Dennis a knowing smirk. *Alien 3* trading cards tanking even worse than the xenomorph-wasted snoozefest film itself. "By the way, I found another bagged 75 and tucked it beneath the register if you want to price and sell it."

"It's for R.J. Montella," Stu said, pausing a moment so he didn't lose his current count. "From my personal stash. I'm not worried about doing the guy a solid. I have three more at home, still sealed."

"Ah, I should've known," Chet returned. "Cover price, right? No markup?"

"Correct. Slip it into his pull box."

"Why does everyone fall over themselves for R.J., anyway?" Dennis asked without looking up. He was on copy 37... 38... 39...

"He writes for *Village Voice,* duh!" Chet blared with such a screech to his voice he came off like a shameless fanboy.

"The guy drops big money in my store," Stu said with a possessive loft to his voice. He finished the second case and carried a large stack of Superman comics to the foldout table he'd spread out near the front of the store. The table itself was draped with a gaudy, bright red latex tablecloth (a purposeful bloodiness to mark the occasion) and a slate photocopy of the front cover of *Superman* #75. The torn and waving cape looked even more dreadful than it did in color. "He writes about comics aside from music and film. He said he'd mention us sometime if he could find a way to do it. Once this Superman rage dies down, no pun intended, I'd be grateful for the publicity."

"R.J. is a god," Chet fawned, as if the national entertainment writer who lived a mere five minutes away was standing in the store right now to bask in his adulation.

One of the old divinities had possibly taken offense by the mere statement, because the air outside suddenly sounded like it was peeling apart.

Not a mere gust from a vicious winter squall. More like a tinny squeal emitted from the release from a tight stretch of a balloon's intake valve, amplified to ear-splitting cacophony.

FWWWEEEEEEEEEEEEEEEEEEEEEEE!!!!

An explosion worthy of a comic book, worthy of the Superman-Doomsday arc itself, rocked the shopping center.

Above the panicking crowd, Dennis and his team felt the floor beneath them shake as a score of cars jettisoned into the air, somersaulting before landing in metallic, glass-splintering crunches on top of other cars.

For the split second he could process it, Dennis breathed in relief he'd been forced to park so far from the store.

"Fuck me!" Chet screamed, reaching out to both of his blind spots to connect with either of his co-workers. In his dress shirt and shadowy tie, his flapping looked more comical than frantic. Chet managed to swat Stu's wrist before he put his arms back down. "Did I really just see that?"

"Y-yeah," Stu stammered, adding stupidly amidst the echoes of instant devastation, "Holy schnikes!"

Fireballs and detonations arose from the pulverized parking lot with curls of orange and blackened combustion. Car alarms rang everywhere. People in other parts of the shopping center darted around in confusion. Burger King lit up in an inferno like one of their flame broilers had gone rogue.

A backdraft from the pulverized vehicles pushed with such force it knocked most of the people in front of the comic shop against the window. The window itself warped but held in resistance.

Inside Gary's Comics, a quake jiggled the suspended memorabilia. One of the wires holding the Enterprise aloft snapped, and it tipped precariously downwards. Only the second wire stationed on the starship's aft side kept it from taking a warp speed death dive to the floor.

Two people from the line suddenly caught on fire and they ran helter-skelter, crashing into each other before scattering in opposite directions. Twin blazes of howling agony getting only as far as the perimeter of the wreckage before they flopped to the pavement, momentarily blocked from sight by those closest to the storefront. Those folks banded together, clutching one another, crying, shrieking, a few turning to the men inside with dumbfounded looks.

"Call 911, you idiots!" a tall, gangly twenty-something who'd come from wherever, bellowed at them, slapping on the glass. He was wearing a Washington Capitals hockey jersey instead of comic book chic. A quick turn of his back to check the scene behind him revealed a stitched number 12 and the last name of Bondra across his droopy shoulder blades. "Two people just got set on fire! Whattya waiting for, assholes?"

It was Dennis who took cue, scrambling for the cordless phone behind the register, just as more pounding on the windows followed behind him.

"Open the doors!" someone shouted, echoed by another, joined by the guy in the Capitals jersey.

The parking lot apocalypse now manifested a mysterious, mustard yellow mist outside. Like sulfuric gas. An airborne blister agent swallowed the smoke and fire before it, absorbing the atmosphere itself. The stink of it couldn't be contained by mere glass.

"Smells like the shit plant at North Point blew to hell!" Chet snapped, knowing his comparing the reek outside to the local wastewater treatment facility was in as much bad taste as the scrunching of his face sent back at the people whapping upon the windows.

"The Commies pushed the damn button," Stu whispered, as if the paranoiac age of McCarthyism from the 1950s had become fashionable in the US all over again.

Dennis wasn't surprised to hear Stu's Russian prejudice at play, but he nearly forgot to speak once he heard a female 911 dispatcher ask for the nature of his emergency. She sounded barely older than Dennis himself and her voice was soft, if authoritative. Someone he would've wanted to put face to voice if the world wasn't going batshit crazy.

"Something bad just happened here in the Cranbrook Shopping Center! Really bad!"

"What specifically, sir?"

"Something, I don't know what!" he exclaimed, hoping he hadn't blown out the eardrum of the dispatcher, also knowing she probably dealt with such rending decibels twenty times or more a day. "It fell from the sky, like a bomb! It touched down in the parking lot, blasting a whole bunch of cars to pulp! Two people that I could see got killed the blast! They were on fire, oh God, I can't believe I'm saying it! Now I'm seeing nothing but yellow outside and everyone's losing their minds! You gotta send someone down here now!"

Just as Dennis relayed all of this, he saw more people outside pounding on the glass. No longer pleading. Demanding. Like they would stop pushing and smacking and get straight to bashing and busting their way through the windowpanes.

Scary enough, but worse, their skin, no matter the race or hue, had begun to break out in mass bloody blisters.

Even more horrific, their eyes had flushed green inside their sockets.

"Green—" Chet whispered, getting stuck mid-sentence. The sizable Enterprise replica continued to sway hazardously as Chet backed away far enough to avoid its path, should it fall. "How could a person's eyes look like that?"

"Let us in, you bastards!" blared Fatso Father, Harold Hemlich.

Fat or not, Harold had a firm grip on the front door, tugging and tugging. His kid was sunk to his knees, his globby face plastered grossly against the glass door his father was yanking on. The kid looked paralyzed even as his plump cheeks bounced on and off the glass.

Someone else, detectable only by a shroud of his sand-colored whitey afro, managed to latch his meaty arms around Harold's girth and helped him pull.

To Dennis, the cordless felt like it had grown ten times heavier as his call was abruptly cut off, the phone line dead.

The door lock's resistance was nearly a thing of the past until both men wrenching on it fell to the ground. They were overwhelmed by others who'd been waiting in line and newcomers from other stores, sinking their fingers into their mouths, nostrils and eyes. Harold Hemlich disappeared from sight, then his butterball son.

The yellow fog trickled and tumbled around the gory sight of blood spurting and vomit carrying a color no human, could possibly extol. The sludge belching from those doing the ripping and tearing of human flesh was both green and red. An unholy Christmas tinted churn worthy of Krampus as much as Pezazu.

"Oh, my fucking God!" Chet exclaimed.

"Help us!!!" screeched a woman holding her unconscious son, who had to be no older than ten, decked in a long-sleeved shirt bearing a facsimile of The Joker from *The Killing Joke* (a one-shot Batman story nearly as much a craze in 1988 as The Death of Superman now) holding his hands overtop his harried head. Scores of nattering "HA HA HA HA HAs" danced around the tee. Blood and outrageously-colored barf was slung across it.

The entire scene of carnage was a real-life representation of something The Clown Prince of Crime might have engineered himself if Gotham City were an actual living place.

Both the woman and her passed-out child were whisked from sight by blistering hands tearing them to pieces. Their blood fountained and slung lurid streaks across the windows.

Through the yellowish haze emerged a sea of glowing green eyes. Behind them, a faint glimpse of the torched Burger King sign amidst the miasma. The dancing flames would've looked strangely beautiful under less violent scenarios.

"This can't be happening," Dennis said, feeling his mouth hang agape and feeling powerless to shut it the more savage things got outside.

Palms quieted from mashing the window, now sagging downwards with sickening squeaks as those people fell to their gruesome demise.

In their place were green-eyed, skin-chewed zombies belching their hideous gruel, adding to the blood sprayed upon the windows. Distorted and bubbled fists walloped the windows, rippling them, straining them, but not yet successfully shattering them.

"They're gonna get in!" Chet yelped. "What do we do, Stu?"

"Goddamn Soviets were lying!" Stu barked. "Perestroika, my ass! Gorbie's been faking all this time!"

"Are you out of your mind, Stu?" Chet shouted back, "There's no Soviet Union anymore and we'd all be ashes right now if it was a nuke! This — *this* is every apocalyptic nightmare we've been reading in comic books all our geek lives! Alan Moore himself couldn't write this kind of —"

"Jesus wept, the kid's bringing up Alan Moore in the middle of a holocaust!" Stu hollered, gyrating his arms up in the air haplessly. "If Jesus Christ is the Messiah — and I was raised on the Torah instead of King James — then let Him come save our sorry asses right here and right now, in the hour of our inglorious deaths! Baruch Hashem!"

"You're the owner, Stu! Do we let 'em in?"

"Hell no, we don't! Would *you* let a bunch of bleeding pus bags with green eyes inside your front door? Maybe offer them a beer and a game of Parchesi? You've been toking and listening to Pink Floyd too much in your downtime, Chet!"

"You're a murderer!" Chet hissed back at him. "I also quit!"

"If we live long enough, I'll fire you before you get the chance! Now both of you fart heads, gimme a hand! We need to pull those free-standing racks over and block the windows before those mutants start breaking them!"

"Like that's gonna stop them?" Dennis protested, finally getting his bearings. "You maybe want to offer them the second print 75s for free and call it a wash, while we're in the middle of trying to survive?"

"You're *also* fired, smart ass!" Stu barked, jamming his left forefinger toward Dennis with indignance. It reminded Dennis crazily, of all things at this unviable orgy of slaughter, the flint-haired, Spiderman-bashing editor of *The Daily Bugle*, J. Jonah Jameson.

"This really *is* doomsday," Chet said with a tone of finality, as he trotted over to the wooden stock rack where Stu was already shoving from the opposite end. Comic books fell all over the floor, bending and creasing upon impact. Money-minded comics collectors would bemoan the immediate depreciation.

"We'll be sure to thank Dan Jurgens and Roger Stern if we get through this alive," Stu rumbled through his grunts. He ceased his shoving now that he had a second hand. "You get that side, Chet. Dennis, what the absolute hell are you doing? Get over here!"

The thunking across the glass was growing more forceful, along with the roars of cataclysm. The accompanying smell was circulating a full rot from the whirlwind of slaughter.

Dennis' stomach trembled again upon the sight of a muscular, green-eyed grotesquery in blood-slinging berserker mode. The one-time human was clawing at everyone around him. Even tearing up other zombies taking over the shopping center. Dennis whimpered then sprinted away from the sight of green eyes and charred teeth, quickly vanishing in a brutal neck twist.

Dennis was so quick in his haste to reach Stu and Chet he'd inadvertently stomped upon the dumped over comic books. Many tore or crinkled to oblivion as the slippery scatter sent Dennis up into the air, landing square upon his butt and lower back.

"That's coming out of your paycheck!" Stu bellowed as he and Chet inched and wriggled the shelf past the register area.

"Eat shit, Stu!" Dennis hissed, knowing he hadn't been heard. Stu and Chet were desperately trying to hoist the shelf to cover one of the gored-up window panels.

All moot as a horrible peal of breaking glass filled the store.

The stench outside became ten times worse without the barrier. As if North Point's entire slog of human waste had cascaded in a revolting wave of excrement right into Gary's Comics. The xanthous seepage rolled into the shop like a transmuted version of John Carpenter's *The Fog*.

It was the zombie gone wild who'd led the charge and now he had a hold of Stu faster than any of them could've imagined.

Stu's horrified sobs turned into an awful gagging as his mouth was being pried apart by the zombie leader. Just that fast, Stu's jaw was torn off, his liquid screams announcing the severing of it. His disconnected jaw twirled and bounced off Chet's right cheek before Chet himself discovered he possessed a falsetto worthy of those hair metal bands, who'd likewise seen their final hour.

Same as Chet himself, who was tackled and disemboweled before Dennis' eyes.

Dennis' last thought before the horror came for him next, was the green eyes all around him looked just like kryptonite.

Behind the Shadows

Behind the shadows of late dusk in August lies a splinter of evil so perverse, Kent's desperation to quell its insatiable urges has been his continual bane for nearly three years, since he'd run afoul of the incarnate passing him the curse.

The taste of gore upon his palette has become vile, beyond the pale. As unendurable as the labored, bone-twisting metamorphosis itself.

"I know why you're here," Kent mutters to the newcomer barging through the door to his study in a two-level Tudor which had belonged to his father and his father's father. "Tonight's a sturgeon moon. Red, a green corn moon. You've done your homework and you found me. For this, I am content. Happy, even."

"Reprehensible initiate of the devil!" Kent hears before he sees the clenched teeth and the faint trace of a beard wriggling furiously beneath it. Light scarring beneath the bottom lip, as if cut by a straight razor shaving. Or worse. Carrying a hateful snarl of vengeance revealing its intent before the musket's point emerges into the sparse candlelight.

"If you're this clever, I'll trust you've taken the liberty of using silver. It's the only way, my friend."

"Don't call me your friend, you obscene bastard."

"Figure of speech," Kent sighs, glancing at the glass carafe half-filled with single malt Scotch on the table next to his favorite sitting chair. An empty highball glass sits next to it, stenciled with a run of gold-embossed Celtic knots around the rim. "You're entitled to your —"

"Be that as it may, Mr. Moore," Kent hears as the barrel of the musket pokes closer toward him, the flickering lowlight licking around the cold steel. The closer his visitor emerges from the canopy of darkness from the opposite side of his study, Kent finally says his name.

"Jackson Cleary," Kent utters, taking another glance at the Scotch. It calls to him, summoning him to pour a dram, though he knows it would take a fill on high to have any impact. He's not interested in getting drunk, not in the conventional way to numb from life's problems.

I'm the only thing stopping you from killing again, something ethereal to personify the Scotch whispers in a liquid cadence only Kent can hear.

Only when Kent imbibes the Scotch like a tavern drunk, does the beast stay dormant. Claws staved, fangs retracted, tartars checked. The beast appeased. Had this unexpected but not unwelcome encounter never occurred, Kent would already have three full glasses slugged down. Inebriated, dulled, deadened. The adrenaline checked down each cycle. So long as he drinks the Scotch in hurried rounds, before the conversion can take him.

Those times he'd been without Scotch or any hard liquor on-hand, however —

"I suppose we should both be gladdened it's not yet October and the hunter's moon. I've done enough stalking by travel moons, I should wager. All of it being a season of death for me, I'm afraid."

"We had our entire lives ahead of us, you monster," Cleary growls down at Kent, training the rifle straight between the eyes. "Our entire lives!"

"For the unimaginable pain I have caused you, I am truly sorry, Mr. Cleary," Kent sighs, feeling the tremors already building inside of his ankles, his knees, his calves. Presumed quakes working themselves up his body.

Take a drink from me, you fool! Kent hears, knowing it's the decanter given phantom voice, not the Scotch itself. *Another after that. Quickly! Before it happens again!*

"Tell that to Georgina!" Cleary screams at Kent, pulling the musket away long enough to lean forward and shove his face directly into Kent's. "You didn't have to bury her in pieces as I did, Moore! You didn't have to search the entire acreage of our property in search of her legs, her hands, her *head!!!* I know what you are, fiend, but can you even surmise how you hacked my wife to pieces, leaving me to retrieve her, part by part? Georgina's mother and father had no chance to say goodbye to her properly! I could never have stomached them finding her the way *I* did!"

"You are right to feel —"

"By the time I found her head, it was slashed four threads across!" Cleary barked in interruption. "Her torso — you abysmal villain — I haven't slept properly in fortnights! I see the carnage you wrought upon my Georgina every single night! Any sleep *you* get is more than you deserve."

The tears grease Jackson Cleary's cheeks, the slickness leaking down to his chin. He looks sickly and exhausted and the bouncing light by flame makes his grief look even more tragic. The snot bubbling then popping out of Cleary's nostrils are all Kent can stand.

"No man, woman or child should endure such terror!" Cleary shrieks. "I never believed in demons or archangels, and I certainly never believed the lycanthrope was a tangible pestilence haunting the earth, but I know better now! Oh, I know, since I witnessed your final indignity cast upon my beautiful wife! She'd just become pregnant with our child, Moore! *Our child!* It wasn't enough you'd slashed her to pieces. You nosed down at her womb, as if sensing the life growing there!"

Now it was Kent feeling his eyes flood as the recount of his violent measures stung him. Never had anyone until now, brought the horror he'd inflicted back onto his doorstep. It was the first time anyone had put things together. Kent Moore, insurance agent, a seller of life indemnities of all incredible things! Nobody in all of Wetherby fathomed Kent Moore was secretly a werewolf.

"You swine, you ate into her womb! You devoured the fetus!!!"

"Dear God," Kent squeaked, letting his own tears fall, the sight of the Scotch inside his decanter even waterier than it already was. "Cleary, I have wronged you in such fashion, I cannot—"

"No, you cannot!!!" Cleary bellowed into Kent's face, his saliva branding Kent's sullen cheeks before he retracted and swung the musket back into place, this time pressing against Kent's skin. "If there is something, *anything* in this horrid reality worse than death, it's what you've well warranted! I hate you, Moore, with all I have left inside of me!"

The trembling in Kent's legs were growing more intense. He could feel the knotting of the tendons, the cramping of his musculature. The legs were always the first part of the transformation, and it was coming, gnawing, reaching for his abdomen. By the time it seized his guts, then his torso, there'd be no stopping it. The beast would be free once again.

You've been through this before, the carafe pricked at Kent. *Show Cleary you can curb it. The beast doesn't need to come. Drink, man, drink! Hurry, before it's too late! You know what this man means to do!*

"So be it," Kent muttered, wincing from the contracting inside his legs. They grew thicker, the bulging strain ripping through his suit pants. Sprouts of slate tinted hair erupted where fabric once was. "Cleary's wrath is just. Let him know vengeance this night. I've no longer the will to live."

"Who the bloody hell are you talking to, madman?" Cleary demanded, his trigger finger quivering as much as Kent's legs, it appeared. Cleary's eyes, still caught within the candle's glint, grew wide to behold the mutation tearing apart Kent's clothes, his pants before his undergarments. Slitting all of it gone all the way to his waist, exposing an entire new form of fur-based nudity.

"RRRRRAAAAAAAAGGGH!!!" Kent thundered as the torment of his change seared through him. Dense hair still not enough to hide his engorged genitals, Kent felt the throbbing shred through his brain, then flare inside of his eyes which he knew without seeing them, had distorted into a garish yellow. It was the palette overtaking his study, the musket. Cleary himself.

"Sweet Jesus in heaven," Cleary whispered, his trigger finger trembling in fear. He appeared labored, as if the musket's stock had grown ten times in weight and he struggled to keep the barrel trained against Kent's forehead. In fact, it danced between Kent's eyebrows, already gnarling as a grayish-black pelt sprouted all over Kent's contorting face.

"Please look inside your broken heart to find forgiveness and deliver me from this hell, Cleary," Kent managed to grunt out before his nose horribly induced forward with his jawline. A desperate push to remain coherent before losing full control of himself. "I pray you loaded it up with a silverrrrr baaaaallllllllll— ARRRRROOOOO!!!"

"Hell is where you belong, spawn of Satan," Cleary uttered, now with conviction, steadying his aim as Kent's study rang with a clamor it had never before heard, even from the prior generations occupying the same upholstered chair as he.

Kent's blood splattered the chair's pattern of English lions, Medieval shields and plumed knight helmets before dotting the decanter next to him.

"What, by God, does silver have to do with anything, you lunatic?" Cleary muttered, turning his back to Kent's unchecked, bleeding form, already healing itself.

Secrets

1982

"I know you and your mother have a secret."

Jessica nearly dropped the stack of split wood pieces she was struggling to maintain inside her reedy thirteen-year-old arms. She tried to hide her wincing from a splinter now wedged inside her left palm. It hurt her something terrible, like the time she was dared by Casey Putnam to put out her hand overtop a lit Bic. She hadn't touched that hypnotic flame wriggling between Casey's crunched thumb and forefinger, but it had felt like she had anyway. Of course, Casey and that blue Bic he always kept inside of his jeans pockets was far away right now. On the opposite end of the United States.

Jessica didn't want to shame herself in front of her father, a man she viewed as tougher than those loudmouthed professional wrestlers with such cracked monikers as Blackjack Mulligan, "Superstar" Billy Graham and George "The Animal" Steele, whom Daddy either cheered for or roared at in laughter on Saturday afternoons. Jessica would put her father against any of those bellowing gorillas in their circus tights and bozo boots. Her daddy had survived Vietnam, after all.

"I don't know what you mean, sir," Jessica answered him with a shudder she could've blamed upon the nip in the Montana air, much less the nip inside her palm. It was the same sting when Casey would hurl her a spitball on the Rosedale Center Middle School diamondback in Maryland. The fact he'd let her use his padded catcher's mitt only meant he could throw as hard as he wanted, girl or not.

She missed Casey, as she did the reliable mainstay of chirping robins, starlings, and blue jays and the hovering warmth battling a determined chill through much of October. Back in Maryland. Not this place, which had ten times more wildlife on the move and temperatures much colder than what she was used to. Already the grizzly bears and bobcats she'd seen prowling from a distance frightened the bejeesus out of her.

"Hmmph," ruffed the burly elder who'd let himself go unshaven the past couple weeks since they'd moved to Kalispell. He gave his daughter an appraising glance from the corner of his right eye, which peered off-kilter more than it used to back on the east coast. Shifty, like Casey once said about a creepy kid named Karl Fusco at Rosedale Middle. The way Karl obsessively flicked the switch of his pocketknife open and shut around the halls in school, he was someone Jessica was more than happy to have at her back.

"I'm being honest, sir, I really don't."

Jessica hated herself for lying as much as she hated the splinter and worse, hated being so far away from Casey. Casey would eventually forget her since there was Vivian Moore and her blossoming boobs to drool over. Yet Jessica knew Vivian was no fan of baseball. If Vivian Moore had been asked to navigate the arc and adjust the catching mitt for a 70-mile-an-hour sinker, Casey would've found much less to drool over. That boy loved the game more than anything, even chasing girls. Not once had Casey put a move on Jessica and a part of her still hurt over it.

"Selective memory is more like it," Jessica's father noted, the bushy, sandy curls above his upper lip flouncing. He hoisted the silver-flinted axe in a fluid arc around his shoulders, further broadened in their new environment, before bisecting another hunk of future firewood into halves. The air around him smelled of cleaved bark and pine needles. That much of the relocation to Kalispell agreed with Jessica. This had been their fourth rushed move in Jessica's thirteen years, and she knew the reason for immediate haste was valid each time.

Just never out of Maryland before and never this far away.

The nip in the air, the chiseling of her father's torso and biceps, plus his uncharacteristic bristling beard had made the Vietnam veteran more grizzled than before the move. The crackles at the corners of his eyes and his replacement of once-omnipresent white Fruit of the Loom tees with arboreous flannel shirts could make Jessica's dad pass for a lifer lumberjack. The effortless way he pounded tree sections into smaller portions scored an even bigger point had he wanted the claim.

Jessica calling her father "sir" was a prerequisite, though never "ma'am" for her mother. If any concession had been made over the years, it was Jessica's purging "mommy" from her vernacular two years ago to a more adult shortening of "ma."

Compliments came from Jessica's dad as frequently as a pack of Topps or Fleer baseball cards containing any players from her favorite team, the Minnesota Twins. The frustrating hunt for an elusive Kent Hrbek card for the '82 MLB season had persisted coast-to-coast from drops into convenience stores along the two-and-a-half-day trek out west.

Instead of Kent Hrbek, Jessica had scored unwanted triples of Mike Schmidt, Dale Murphy, and Cal Ripkin, Jr.

Since the move to Kalispell, not a friend in sight to swap with, much less anyone who spoke the language of baseball. As it was, the nearest neighbor, the Applebee's, was a mile away; a *country* mile, as they called it around here. Their kids, two boys, had flown the coop for the Air Force Academy in Colorado Springs.

Two weeks after moving almost 2,200 miles to the peculiarly-named Flathead County, Jessica was missing more than her former life. Casey was a New York Yankees fan, whom Jessica hated more than Barbie dolls and toy Easy Bake ovens. Yet Casey always had a spare Rod Carew, Gary Ward, and Doug Corbett double to part ways with and always a *gimme*, never a trade. He was the best friend she'd ever had, even with Casey's contention Rollie Fingers could land outside edge curves far better than Brad Havens, the Twins' strikeout master. *Yeah, right.*

Letting her auburn ponytail swish back and forth from the eructed end of her Twins ball cap, Jessica was missing Casey for reasons other than their shared love of baseball.

"A secret is a secret, but in this family, we *have* no secrets," rumbled the sinewy man who looked far more at home in the raw Montana fall instead of the sometimes-humid regions of the Mid-Atlantic he'd transplanted their family from. "With all we've been through, Jessica, I expect you to remember that."

All summer long, Jessica's dad had been dealing with his night terrors, as he'd called them, with noticeable shame and fear. The other word for his out-of-nowhere panic attacks coming anywhere between 1 to 4 am was "PTSD." Not so much a word, but a — what did those fat, old fogey English teachers in Maryland call it? An acronym, that was it. It stood for "post-traumatic syndrome disorder," and was said to be common amongst soldiers of war.

"The only secret we've had, Dad, I mean, *sir*, is the time Ma and I hid that banjo from you two Christmases ago. After all those dummy gifts of Frosted Flakes, Pork and Beans, YooHoo, and Nyquil, the look on your face when you got the banjo was worth it."

"Don't patronize me with smart-aleckiness, young lady," Jessica's father went on, without looking at his daughter. "And don't you dare take me for a fool. I've seen better liars calling the shots from Washington, DC during the Easter Offensive."

The axe swung in a precise, ovular rhythm as Jessica's father kept chopping at the vast pine tree sprawled before his mud-caked work boots. To look at him go, one would never have known the family had slugged through winters in Maryland in less rugged fashion through oil heating, then baseboard.

Montana had already changed Jessica's father, as it was quickly changing Jessica herself. Casey had always called her a tomboy back home. Her prior home. He'd done so last year after his mother took both to see *The Empire Strikes Back* and Jessica had muttered "Kick that Stormtrooper in his tin-plated nuts, Chewie," as Darth Vader plunged Han Solo into carbon freeze in such morbid fashion. Stinking Vader. Jessica always wondered what kind of kid he'd been at some earlier time in a galaxy far, far away.

If only Jessica's mother had been there with them at the movies. Of course, there was a reason Jessica hadn't invited Ma invited along. Made the excuse Ma had been dealing with a fever, which was a complete fib.

The same night, after seeing *Empire,* had been one of the worst at the Rosedale house. It was hard for Jessica not to think of Boba Fett, Bossk, and those butt-ugly alien bounty hunters in the same thread as the horror show she'd endured later in the evening. They were tamer, though. *Much* tamer.

"I'm not sure what patronize means," Jessica said to her father, trying to remove any trace of smart-aleckiness from her response.

"Never mind that," her father said with a brusque, dismissive shake of his head.

Each strike of the axe exposed more of a dense essence, filling the crisp air around them as Jessica's father sectioned off the wood for Jessica to carry away. To Jessica, the split wood she transported to the right side of their new, log-sided home registered the combined pong of wet leaves and an extinguished campfire.

An earthy ruddiness, which reminded Jessica she'd yet to be taken as promised by her father, to Glacier National Park, only a twenty-minute drive away. Even with goofy-sounding points of interest inside the stunning Glacier National Park ecosystem like Polebridge, Babb, and Wild Goose Island. They'd been as much a selling point to the move for Jessica as the main reason for their rush out of Maryland.

However, the family had stayed inside their new home every weekend thus far.

Jessica and her father had absorbed the brunt of the settling and unpacking to the point where all the cardboard boxes had been flattened and bundled into the storage shed with only a riding mower the prior owner had left for them. Also, her father's axe.

Ma had devoted Saturday and now Sunday, to baking, canning, and making preserves for the slim pantry cabinet already stuffed with flour, sugar, seasonings, and pancake mixes. Ma had dished up iron-griddled blueberry flapjacks, which Jessica's father loved, even if the tart pancakes had lost their luster on Jessica herself. A box of Captain Crunch was still in the pantry closet, down to a quarter full. Jessica had taken to rationing her cereal, given the nearest supermarket was a full fifteen-minute drive away. The Pantry Pride back in Rosedale was so close, Jessica could've walked back and forth, and she often did.

Right now, Jessica's mother was in bed after having one of her shit-hit-the-fan (her father's favorite off-color saying) episodes while washing the dishes. Episodes, in Jessica's mind, far worse than her dad's PTSD, though she had the furthest clue what awfulness he'd seen in 'Nam.

All Jessica had to go on in life was what was smack in front of her. Especially her mother's frequent tendency to freeze in place, clutch the sides of her head, and shriek like a thousand volts of electricity were plowing into her. Then what came afterwards. It wasn't for anyone but Jessica and her father to know, much less repeat.

This time when the incident happened after breakfast, Jessica's mother took one of the plates and smashed it over the side of the sink, before picking up a shard and aiming the tip toward her wrist. It had taken both Jessica and her father to subdue Ma in her desperation to slash herself. Jessica's dad was right now wearing an unseen band-aid over the gash he'd taken from his wife earlier, who'd squealed into his face, full of transformative fury, "I don't want this anymore! Let me do it!"

By now, Jessica had stopped crying whenever her mother had one of those spastic freakouts. A numbness had, of late, pervaded Jessica every time Ma turned into —

"I know life's harsher out here than what you're used to," Jessica's father broke into her roaming thoughts, ceasing his revolutions and letting the axe head rest next to his work boot, the handle against his leg. Both limbs seemed to have grown thicker over a month's time. "I'll take *this* over the Francis Scott Key Bridge and Harbor Tunnel back in Baltimore. I don't miss the traffic jams and the tailgaters. Well, there're tailgaters out here too, especially when the locals spy an out of state license plate.

Here I thought driving an F-150 would've made us accepted de facto."

"You can count the number of cars coming down the hill," Jessica said, grateful to be let off the hook. "Most of them are pickups like ours. They sure do love their trucks out here."

The splinter was still making its irksome presence known in her hand. If only she could excuse herself without answering a litany of questions, to find a sewing needle from Ma's basket, wherever it had gone to into this new cabin-house. Jessica would pluck the insidious thing out herself and then squib a hit of Bacitracin afterwards. Like her mother used to do, before the episodes started happening. What Jessica had never known until a couple years ago, was her mother had been dealing with the episodes her entire life. They were just now getting beyond her capability to stop from coming.

Having something else to talk about helped pull Jessica's attention away from the splinter until she could go inside. She would have to remember to burn the tip of the needle first to avoid infection from digging beneath the skin. Jessica wished Ma was who she used to be when Jessica was six years old. Steady and confident, strong and gentle in the same swoop. Someone to be trusted with a sharp object.

"How many did you count in just the past hour?"

Now Jessica's father looked amused instead of put-out, as he addressed her. She knew his facial and body rhythms like she knew Bobby Castillo's screwball was to be reckoned with at the plate. Jessica wished Casey would've kissed her goodbye, but he could have Rollie Fingers and his silly curlicue mustache all he wanted.

Enough pining over stupid Casey and stupid Maryland, Jessica admonished herself. *If you're lucky,* really *lucky, you*

*may run into Casey sometime, somewhere on a vacation, not that
we take those anymore, since Ma —*

"Earth to Jess."

Jessica snapped out of her reverie. Now she could see
her father, here in pre-winter Kalispell, Montana, where
geese turds were rumored to freeze in mid-drop.
Considering what only happened a couple hours ago in the
kitchen, he was remarkably calm.

"I counted eight," Jessica said, ready with her answer
as promptly as her zillionth dignitary salutation, "sir."

"Yup, you can hear the fish do their dirty business
down at the lake, this place is so quiet," her father told her
with a sudden flush to his cheeks Jessica knew had nothing
to do with the bitter Montana air. "The grizzlies, too,
though I'm sure they're much rowdier with their dirty
business if they haven't hibernated already. You don't
have to tell Ma I said any of that."

"But wouldn't that be a secret?"

The sudden scrunching of his cheeks and a warning
shot from his crinkling pupils told Jessica she'd treaded the
line, a line marked without question or argument of what
constituted "smart-aleckiness."

"Little lady, that'll be enough," Jessica's father
commanded, though she detected more restraint than his
usual correcting of her. "Chasing caribou out of our trash
is less of a hassle than you are right now."

"Yes, sir," Jessica conceded, dipping her head, trying
not to proclaim the disturbance she felt. Ma was dead to
the world, if not dead inside already, doped up on a valium
cocktail. If only there was something Jessica could do to
make it all go away. To cure her mother. That meant much
more than finding a Kent Hrbek card.

"The TV reception's lousy out here, sure," her father
went on, gently tapping the axe head with his boot in
repeated knocks. "The rabbit ears are next to worthless in

the mountains and if I have to hear your mother squawk one more time how she's missing *Soul Train,* but I get to watch the WWF, I'm going to split my head apart with this thing before it touches another piece of lumber."

This made Jessica giggle.

"We get all the action we want here in the yard, though," her father rambled. "Squirrels, mountain cottontails, coyotes, red foxes, and raccoons, plus mule and white-tailed deer. You saw those flattened along the 695 Beltway more than alive back in Maryland. I keep the Polaroid within reach on my nightstand whenever those grizz and black bear show up, but I'm not hopeful of getting a picture. Not one I'd want to get too close to. Then those dratted milk snakes we've already gotten more than I care to see. Nearly as many pit vipers, banded kraits, and Chinese cobras I ran across in the 'Nam."

"I remember you teaching me about the difference between diamond heads and the rounded head snakes," Jessica blurted. She did so as much to contend with the splinter pain and her worries over Ma, as to impress her father. "The spoon shapes aren't poisonous."

"Very good," her father said, and Jessica took full document of his praise as the instant treasure it was.

Jessica smiled back at her father, swinging her arms behind her back, locking her hands overtop her butt. Somehow, this alleviated some of the splinter's bite.

"Still, it's always best to stay on the safe side when it comes to snakes and assume the worst. I'll never forget that riled-up cobra testing my unit's resolve under cover, where you didn't dare move. This with the enemy positioned maybe a quarter of a mile away from us."

"I'd pee myself," Jessica blurted, shocked at her own forwardness. If her father had found any offense by it, he'd let it slide. In fact, he'd creaked an unexpected smirk.

"A few of us did just that, once the cobra raised its hood at us," Jessica's dad said with enough evenness for her to know he was speaking in earnest.

"Did you?"

"That's *my* secret," he replied, jerking his eyebrows up and down as a lark. "In keeping with the situation, as Charles Dickens once wrote. I guess now's a good time as any for a little spillage of the war days. Ma knows all of it, but I don't talk about it in front of her much anymore. For obvious reasons."

"I suppose so," Jessica said, hoping her sudden surprise was visible as she felt it spread across her face. She'd seen more on *This Week in Baseball* to pull her cheeks apart in wonderment at plays of the week, the rare triple play and 405 feet dingers which seemed weird in domed coliseums instead of open-air ballparks. What her father just now said was like a forbidden book suddenly unlocked before Jessica's eyes.

"I watched guys in the company slip around in the guts of our blown-to-bits brothers." Jessica's father sighed, looking toward the cluster of spruce and ponderosa pine lining the steep driveway spelunking from their steeped new home to the thoroughfare below.

Jessica saw the steam cloud around her dad's head like a mystical haze as he exhaled, no doubt gathering thoughts he wished he could forget.

"In the 'Nam, we were dodging napalm showers which didn't see the difference between the Cong and G.I. Joes. I heard orders passed from inexperienced West Point graduates being passed bullshit orders from bullshit bureaucrats and five-star Pentagon jockeys too porky to remember what a Cammie and ALICE feels like, much less reliable intel. The blame game went all around, but the effects fell upon rangers in the field, sent to die before anyone with a row of bullshit service medals took accountability. We *won* that war, Jessica, never forget it. Excuse my language."

"No, sir," she said dutifully without meaning to interrupt him. "Never."

"That's my girl. We won Vietnam, no matter what the news reporters at home said, or whatever the draft-dodging hippie-dippies felt. We lost in the way that hurts most, as in the casualties, the ones who showed up for Basic and hula-hooped the oncoming bullets instead of burning their draft cards. Makes me sick to think how many punched their ticket from the Cong and how many capable bodies kicked up in leather back chairs, let us do it for them."

Jessica was within reach of asking why a person not putting his life on the line for war could be considered lesser, but she silenced her lips. The splinter especially, shut her up with its return throb.

"When left to our devices and with a competent command," her dad continued, still glancing more at the timbered estate than her, "Victor Charlie took it far worse than we did. Most of the time, anyway. We called them 'gooks,' 'slants,' 'boys in black pajamas.' They fought like hell; you can't take that away from them. We had a peculiar respect for people we were taught to hate and to kill on sight. We could've shared beers and goddamn *joints* with the VC under other circumstances, they were that tough and shrewd. Those tough and shrewd bastards claimed victory at Khe Sanh, though our air cover wiped those grinning gooks off the shitting map at Ia Drang. Khe Sanh, *nobody* wants to relive that mess. Excuse my language again, young lady, but *fuck* the United States government. I would've pissed on Johnson's grave if Texas wasn't so far out of our way during the move."

"I'm sorry you had to go through that, Dad, I mean, sir," Jessica quipped, letting her father know, by silent sapience, it was okay his lexicon had exceeded the boundary set between father and child.

"I joined the Army to make my father proud," Jessica's own replied, thrusting his chest out no doubt the same way he did back in June of 1965, recounting his enlistment date. "I did and *didn't* want his Bronze Star. I got one of my own, thank you, fucking Cong, though I've only pulled it out for your mother to see. I also got the Purple Heart."

"Isn't that for when you get hurt in war?"

"Jess, you make me happier than I may let on. Yes, dear girl, that's exactly what a Purple Heart is."

"What happened to you, sir? I mean, you're so strong."

"Strength is only one part of being a solider, baby girl."

There was a sudden warmth to her dad's projection which not only generated steam against the compressed cold, it engulfed his entire head as it filtered. It gave Jessica the courage to ask him, "How so?"

"First off, Jess," her father said, letting go of the axe handle. It seemed like a slow drop to Jessica's eyes before it struck the hard, frozen earth. The impact sound was unlike what she expected. It sounded hollow, like barren finality. "You can dispense with the formalities."

"I don't understand, sir," Jessica said, curiously, not caring if it made her seem dense.

"Drop the word 'sir,' when you address me," Jessica's dad said, placing a hand upon her left shoulder. The exertion with the grasp behind his intended affection felt nearly as assuring as the time she'd brought home all Bs on her final fifth grade report card at Essex Elementary School. "There's an old saying from the military, 'Don't call me 'sir,' I work for a living.'"

"But you finished as a lieutenant," Jessica protested, knowing by instinct how much dispute to fill her voice with.

"Which makes me a non-commissioned officer. You're intelligent beyond your years, Jess, but let's not worry over semantics, alright? 'Dad' will suffice from here on out, does that work?"

"Okay," was all Jessica could come up with, wanting to throw her arms around her father for multiple reasons, but for just as many, she kept them locked behind her back.

"I'm not gonna lie, Jess, I'm worried this time about your mother."

"I have been for a long time, sir, I mean, Dad."

Her father sent back a silent, shaky grin to serve as his agreement before telling her, "When we're finished, show me what's wrong with your hand. I see you favoring it."

Jess returned the same facial ease his way and for a moment all seemed right in Montana.

"EEEEEEEEEEEEYYYYYYAHHHHHHHH!"

"Oh, Jesus!" Jessica's father snapped in reaction to the shrill yelp, before bursting toward the front door.

He needn't have bothered since the door groaned beyond its hinges from a violent force. Instead of easing shut, the top hinge exploded and teetered from that point, refusing to close.

What was supposed to be Ma, was anything but.

The only telltale sign was the floral print nightgown and the same ruddy hair she'd passed on to her daughter, looking like it had been blown to hell inside a wind tunnel. The nightgown itself, shredded from neckline to the abdomen, like the wearer had torn it in a haste to be free of the confinement. The face, contorting and bending with audile stretching and tearing of cartilage overtop a skull hyperextending from the nose and chin. A briny, pink slobber oozed from elongating jowls, not so much like a row of incisors; her jawline bore sickening, jagged shards capable of slicing through almost anything they wanted.

Worst was the expansion of Ma's eye sockets as if viciously pried apart by an unseen entity taking savage delight in the splitting, then the blackening of the pupils inside.

"Riiiiiichaaarrrrrrd —" hissed the thing both Jessica and her father referred to as "Ma," despite the garish miscreation lurking inside of her, set free once again.

"Dear God, Jolene, no!" Jessica's father bellowed, sending a nearby jackrabbit bolting as if a wooded Armageddon was hot on its cotton-balled tail.

The atrocity which had done so much damage to the front door, which had wanted to slit its own wrist this morning and which had transmuted into something amphibian, mammal, and extraterrestrial all at once, was scampering, not running, toward Jessica's dad. Nowhere near as fast as the sprinting rabbit, the aberration paused only in recognition of its name.

Jolene-that-was snarled its ravening teeth, flash-checking Jessica with something the daughter knew in her normal, mortal form was a *don't even try it* kind of warning. Parental and rigorous despite the driveling mandibles and bulbous eyes, plus breasts which had grown exponentially and now with a repulsive combination of scales and fur sprouts. The unholy spawn of some freakish, Dr. Moreau-esque mongoloid.

Not Ma. A Ma-*Thing*.

"Ma, please don't make me do it," Jessica whispered, feeling instant betrayal as her mother turned her vulgar sights upon her husband.

"Kiiiii… mmmmeeeeee…. Riiiiiicharrrrrrrrrrd…." gurgled the Ma-Thing

Jessica was looking beyond Ma-Thing, spying the discarded axe where her father had tossed it. He was even beginning to give it a precursory glance.

For the first time in Jessica's entire life, she witnessed tears leak down her dad's cheeks. It would've broken her heart straightway any other time.

In this form, the monster Jolene Monica Reynolds became when her adrenal glands flared at their highest, had been responsible for the malevolent deaths of seven people across Maryland within a three-year span.

The move to Kalispell, Montana from Maryland had been a fly-by-night cover up, after Jolene's latest mauling had been a construction worker on his lunch break, a direct attack in a Rosedale mall parking garage. Ma-Thing confessed to her family the following day to having gnawed the guy's innards out and leaving them slung across the pavement. Ma, not Ma-Thing, had sobbed at her powerlessness to control the beast inside of her, which had taken that seventh life, only because she'd gotten into a profane argument with the guy over his flagrant discarding of a hamburger wrapper upon the ground.

The news reports in each case back in Maryland, conveyed a mere portion of the actual gore Ma-Thing had left from her victims. Area detectives only found a "special pink saliva" slung upon each slain corpse. The single link they had, that blush-colored sputum, prompted the vile moniker from the media, "The Maryland Spit Slayer."

It took nothing at all for Ma-Thing to bring down her six-foot-two spouse faster than any cannonade around Da Nang or the conflagration heaped upon the Eliot Combat Base at the DMZ in Vietnam. A decorated, discharged officer had become an enabler for the woman he loved, bearing a horrid secret only he and Jessica shared.

However, Jessica had one more secret and it was time to put it into action.

"Kiiiiii meeeee—" Ma-Thing ralphed into her husband's pinned, roaring face, that nauseating pink drool cascading down his battle-carved cheeks.

"Jolene, I won't!" he yelled back at her, thrusting his gnawed and slimed face toward the ground. "I *can't* do it!"

A sickening *thunk!* tumbled across the ground as Ma-Thing's severed head rolled feet away. If crimson blood could turn into instantaneous bile, this is what gorged out of the sliced end of Ma-Thing's neck, literally vomiting all over Jessica's dad, belching hot hybrid lava into his grief-stricken face.

"No, no, no," he half-moaned, half-choked as the puke-tinted spew sprayed all over him. It was his breaking point, no matter all the chewed-up bodies he'd seen in *Kháng chiến chống Mỹ*, the Vietnamese's so-called "Resistance war against America."

"I'm so sorry, Dad," Jessica wheezed bravely, no tears or immediate anguish, all of which would come later. The hands grasping the axe quaked. The splinter felt ten times worse, as if burrowing itself there for good. Forget the needle, much less a capable hand to free it loose.

"NOOOOOOOOOOOOOOOO!!!" her father roared, shoving the headless body of Ma-Thing off him, the same once-woman whom he'd cherished, made love to, and brought a daughter into the world with.

"She made me promise not to tell you," Jessica said tediously, without remorse. She dropped the axe where she stood, the handle plopping across her right Minnetonka Moccasin. "She knew what she was. Coming out here didn't matter. She knew she'd do it again. Dad, she wanted to die. Please don't hate me."

"You will kill ten of us," Jessica's father uttered, his pupils flaring in shell-shocked devastation. As much as he was mourning his wife on-the-spot, he was back on the front line, quoting former Vietnamese leader, Ho Chi Minh. "We will kill one of you, but in the end, you will tire of it first."

Deepfake

Even with the end of a literal switchblade propped beneath my chin, I couldn't tell you the name of the live streamer pawning wholesale killing.

Problem is, the pitchman not only looks like me, he *is* me. Hacked into a garmented avatar of death.

I've become an e-merchant of slaughter. The robocall doesn't match the moving lips, yet it's my voice, synthetically created, out of progression.

Fragments of pinyin scatter camouflage an auction counter beneath me-not-me, selling murder rights to a sobbing girl offscreen. The bid pushes into seven figure territory.

Helpless, the laptop camera transmutes my dread into virtuality.

Vladana's Daughters

Dracula has crossed death's threshold, yet his pale, unmortal brides remain. A marriage never ordained, but a marriage, nonetheless. I grieve just as much as I want to spit upon the mere mention of his infernal name.

I once longed for the same permanence relieving my former husband from his perpetual thirst. Now I see my unexpected freedom as the gift it is. Liberation? Not quite. However, here lies the opportunity for something more auspicious for Vladana Ćosić, than mere widow to an implied immortal.

Lord Dracula, you absolute fool, a vampire *can* be killed! Let the poetical stylings of Heinrich August Ossenfelder and John Polidori give lilt to gory choruses raised by your romanticized children of the night. What music shall they make now, dear Count?

It's a snow-choked London nocturne with capacious constellations apparent through the tenebrious winter sky as if cloaked across a Yorkshire meadow instead of the grandest municipality in all of Europe. The kind of chilly twilight made for Strigoi encroachments from their hallowed sepultures in Highgate. A generous, moonlight sky, sure to coax the savage rendering of lycanthrope emanations.

A night for jackals, a night for delirium.

A spectacular night to feed.

"God be with you, my lady."

I'm no lady, not in the sense these ignorant English think me to be.

My only complaint about there being a 'God' is in the way these shallow commoners seem no better than the Saxons and Franks who'd butchered one another, centuries ago in the name of conversion. How could their slain and elevated Jesus Christ, who has been said to have died for the world's sins, permit the atrocities committed by such a beast as Dracula, to go without retribution? Much less infect others like me and my former 'sisters?' In our case, imprisoning us with a dowry of blood. That, and countless gold we were denied access to.

I try not to snarl at the plump old geezer bundled tighter than a hot cross bun, trembling inside his shivering hand. A hand growing garish and frostbitten. A pair of gloves is what he needs, as much a gooey bakery good. He is chilled to his aged bones, that much is obvious. Homeless, also apparent. There are lots like him sadly all over London. A scene played on repeat before my eyes, none of it any heartier than my epoch of eternity stowed beneath Castle Dracula.

The rusty, dented cup he's holding in his other hand quakes, and I spot inside it, a grimy coin. A shilling, by measure of the crown's commerce. These are some of the shabbiest people I've seen since my arrival in London less than a week ago. A town my lord had become obsessed with, and unwittingly ushered his undoing.

I nonetheless see Dracula's fascination. So many people inside a packed city, procreating as if civilization itself depended on it. The cries of the babies in London are nearly as shrill as the wolves in Transylvania. I could simply snatch this fodder of the poor into the shadows and feed upon them. People only their fellow destitute would miss.

"Where, then, is God's promised gift of eternal paradise?" I ask the poor wretch, who has every right to eye me quizzically. He should be turning away and tramping for his life through the mud and slush already caked to his tawdry boots. Were I feeling charitable, I have all the money needed to provide him a fresh pair of clothes and a place to stay for a week as my guest at The Governess on Fleet Street. Mine is a drafty room with a single bed and there's an unoccupied duplicate across from me. Unlike my former Lord, I have no need to sleep inside my native dirt, though I can never sleep by moonlight ever again. Seems like infinity since I last walked the earth in daytime hours.

I could clean this disheveled itinerant up with a hot bath and feed him greasy chicken quarters from the innkeeper downstairs. I could bring him desserts far more filling and soppier than the paltry pastry he sustains himself on right now. Black Forest cake, perhaps. Honeyed Hell, I could further sweeten his blood with a carafe of Merlot.

I could do all those things, but I would be no better than my shared mate of the damned, and the way he'd played that young English solicitor, Jonathan Harker, for a dupe. Toying with his food, as it were.

This well-intentioned, if rumpled man, is so old he's hardly worth the effort, as I'm sure he already feels, roving on the streets with nowhere to go and no one to care for him. He's been doing this a long time, I can tell. He's a survivor and yet I can sense his vitality dwindling. To take him in this withered state would be no better than taking a morsel, a snack. A tease.

Only the young can supplicate that which seeps from me, the longer I wait for a proper meal.

I've already had a cat last night, a mature, ash-colored tabby with the misfortune of crossing my path down a quiet dockyard with scant few shipmen to be found attending their commissions. Faster to catch the tom as a Nosferatu than an ordinary mortal could. The tabby's feline blood was hot and savory. I gave it a long chase on purpose, knowing I could've snatched it any time. I let it raise its exertions, making for a deliciously warm appeasement, even if that's all it was in the grand perspective. An appeasement.

"Come again, Lady?" the old man queries, and I halfway feel sorry for him. Normally I don't bother with someone his age, but it's been a fortnight since I arrived in London by way of Whitby. I'm so terribly *hungry,* and not for the nourishments of mortals.

I long for actual sustenance as much as I long for the company of Tatiana and Danica. I miss them greatly and have, more than once, questioned myself for the choice I've made. God or Goddess, or whatever mysterious divinity watches over vampires, look kindly upon my one-time sister brides. Or put an end to their misery.

I would opt for the latter, but I have greater designs with the liberty we've been delivered.

"Certainly not in this arena of bedlam," I say to the hoary, shuddering man, surveying the crowd around us. A mindless herd mindlessly milling. Men tipping top hats with squishy insteps, women muddying the hems of their dress trains through the London town slop.

I no doubt stand out with my golden, curled tresses bouncing in rebellion of the night air and the pinkish rouge flecked upon my cheeks, masking a deadened pallor which would likely send most onlookers in fright. This is no longer the age of those ghastly powdered wigs.

Unlike the ramshackle robes I'd worn with my sister wives beneath Castle Dracula, waiting to be accredited by his presence, much less his offerings of victuals, I am tonight regal. As a consort of the imperial template of vampires should be.

I see nobody watching us, so I gently lift my lips. Were this displaced man in his prime, I might consider bedding him, before dining on him. I still feel something in my feminine private places, a longing to be nurtured only in the way our perished husband could fashion.

To all of us. Usually one at a time, sometimes all three in one session. Usually after Dracula, or one of his wolves brought us an infant from one of the mountain villages to feed upon. Food before sex. Those were the true nights of ecstasy.

"Kisses for all," he used to convey to his brides, no doubt relishing the power he held over us.

I can still hear Dracula whisper into my ear, "You will always be my first and most favorite, Vladana," before flicking his tongue along my earlobe, gliding his incisors down the slope of my whitish jugular ever-so-slightly. Never sinking into me any longer, since he'd already stolen my mortality along with my virginity, more than a century ago. I revere these attentions, despite his outright raping me the first time.

The memory of Dracula's lovemaking tingles, and it has me broiling inside. I want to copulate as much as I want to eat. I would just as soon have felt young Harker between my legs before supping on his sterilized life blood when the moment had presented itself. Mortal man blood spiked with a hormonal fragrance tinging the palette. Only newborns sate greater.

Why must this man before me be so confoundedly *old?*

"Jesus in heaven, no," the man croaks at me, already sounding his demise before I could ever do anything to him. His treat tumbles out of his tremoring hand, and it makes a marshy splat in the mud.

I find it amusing and tragic in the same breath.

I know he sees my fangs and the sudden red flash inside my eyes, because the fop is now crossing himself repeatedly as he backs away, trying not to capsize from his struggling feet.

Now he is bringing unwanted attention and I curse myself for playing my hand too soon. I don't hiss or say anything in his bumbling attempt to repulse me. His salutes to the Christ look more like someone caught in a seizure. Perhaps this was why my departed husband was successful for so many years, until that cur Van Helsing caught up to him.

"Demoness!" the man pushes out of his blubbery, wrinkled mouth, and I quickly pull away from him, trying to blend into a newly arriving bundle of townsfolk.

"Evening, my lady," one of them says, tipping his hat to me in passing. Amazing how they all look like replicates of one another. In dress and in progressions.

"Good sir," I return with a curtsy-on-the-move. On the lam, to be more accurate.

Fortune smiles upon me, even in my error as I hear the same group of people shaming the old man with derogatory street lexicon like "dalcop beggar" and "raggabrash," to the more hostile, if seldom used term from Shakespeare's time, "cumberground." As in someone so immaterial they're simply taking up space in the world.

"Here now, be off, you raving fopdoodle, and leave good, civilized folk alone," I hear with my back turned, smiling broader than I should.

Civilized, how rich.

I haven't been amongst the general population since I was taken from my homeland in Loznica, Serbia. When I think upon Loznica, I must smother the rare yearning for my mother's eggplant and red pepper-based ajvar. It's the garlic cloves in the recipe I can't handle, for obvious reasons.

A busy town even a hundred years ago, Loznica can't hold a candle to London's compact populace, which comes alive by gaslight, even readier than its workaday mechanisms.

A near-flawless habitation for a vampire.

The smells of London are a mad clash of cooked meats, lavender, frankincense, tomato soups, bakery goods, ales, rye whiskeys, freshly caught fish waiting to be purchased, and to the less savory side, human piss and shit. I understand there's a town in England appropriately called Shambles, where the townsfolk dump their excrement and waste into the gutters and let Nature have her will wherever their filth may go.

I see the same here in London, as I see men wander into alleys, not only to relieve themselves, but sometimes to empty their seeds into trollops for a 'joey,' or sixpence in this city's currency. They do it in relative openness to passersby instead of the stew-houses, or brothels, of which there are plenty in this town. The sight of it makes me feel devilish inside, and it gives me ideas for my future. Oh, the delicious prospect of seducing a man on the younger side to have a go with me until *I'm* satisfied, not he, before I feed on him.

Not as delicious as what I spot next.

Or, rather, whom.

I nod to yet another grouping, men escorting their women by the crook of their arms and I'm starting to feel majestic, even with the mud soaking into the bottom of my dress and mucking the heels of my boots. The squashy sounds have grown less comical as my heart accelerates in a way it hasn't felt since back in Transylvania, when our sovereign would bring us nubile feasts. The screeches and caterwauls those babes made as Tatiana, Danica and I drank our fill from them.

I long to hear such turmoil again.

"A one penny, if you please? A tuppence if you can spare?"

Her voice delights me. Her ruddy cheeks, nipped by Winter's cruelty, are adorable, despite the degradation seized upon her. Her bird's nest of brown hair, barely covering ears as red and chapped as her nose—it all screams of suffering.

She's freezing, this child, while I feel nothing of the frost. I've been one with the chill ever since I was dead and reborn. Yet, I know how the pitiful urchin must feel, almost as desperate to exist as the old man, yet nowhere near as seasoned at it as he. She will certainly die, because her coat is beyond tattered and the nightgown, which must have looked as robust as she once did, is pocked full of holes, exposing her abdomen. I know of a few letches from my short time in London who would pay half a crown for unspeakable privileges with her. They make me want to turn those perverted languishers and stake them in the same fell swoop.

Yes, the girl will die, I'm certain. As certain as I know Tatiana this very minute still mourns the loss of our common master. Yet there is a way for this girl to live on. As my handmaiden, of course.

You see, my entire reason for going on as a castaway bride of the prodigious Count Dracula, is I want a coven of my own.

Even when casting a full, white mustache and a sometimes-gaunt exterior, Dracula was the essence of manhood. Shed of those aged exteriors upon feeding from the right man or woman, he was a stunning godhead of the underworld. His domination, his allure, his mesmeric stare, compelling others to bend their knees to him.

I want that, all of it, for myself.

"Poor little poppet," I say to the trembling girl, attempting to use the local vernacular, knowing how it must sound from my foreign tongue. Of course, these Brits sound to me nearly as strange and exotic as their hated enemies, the French. "Why settle for scraps when you can have something as fine as this?"

I pull from my purse a 100-dinar banknote, currency from my motherland, plundered by Dracula along with everything else that was my former life. Unusable in London, not until you visit the exchange and convert it. It's the '100' numeration itself and the alien look to it which has caught the girl's attention. Moreover, her imagination.

Easy prey.

"Whaaaat?" the waif whispers. A cloud of steam emits from the gape of her stunned mouth but the reek of her breath is hardly offensive to one who lives on blood. It stinks, for sure, not unlike the discards of offal behind the butcher shops. I already want her; thus, I want to punish whoever has put this child in such a dire predicament.

"Where are your parents, little dove?" I ask, watching the fledgling squint her eyes at me. If I were to bet on this very banknote, I'd put the girl at age eight. There's mistrust as much as there is curiosity in the youngling's eyes, and I cannot blame her.

"They're gone, mum," she speaks, as high as she dares, pushing her hazel pupils as far toward the right of each eye socket as they can withstand. Suspicious, yet I've found a way past her defenses. "Diphtheria, both. I shan't say no more, other than I'm on my own."

"Aww," I say back, reaching down and caressing the child's knotty hair, trying not to give her anything but a compassionate stare into those apetala eyes which dart in fear of me. Yet signaling of the same excitement I felt when Lord Dracula offered me a warm meal of Serbian Sevapcici, before making me as callous, cold, and sometimes starved as he. I should've taken it as a warning he'd sat at a table away from me until I'd finished eating.

"The city devours those who cannot fight for themselves. I would see you with a proper chance to fight back."

"I can't take this, mum," the girl tells me, and I see something I can only assume is disappointment. "No one would let me buy anything with it, pretty as it is."

"Of course not," I reply, tucking the dinar back into my purse before shaking it so the girl can hear all the local gold pieces jangling inside. "I have more than enough of —"

A cavalier man, no more than his late twenties, I'd wager the same dinar, takes note of our exchange and the heartbreaking frisson of the girl. He interrupts me with a sizeable fist thrust between us.

"Open your hand, love."

As if she hadn't been transfixed enough on me, the girl shifts her gaze to the new arrival, someone I want to pounce upon and sink my ravenous teeth into, because he is as right for me as the girl herself. Even more so.

I'm partially jealous, partially guilty, as he presses a gold guinea piece into the girl's quivering paw.

"These streets are not for one as ye, lass," he says, and I know enough of the world to know this is a visitor to London, as much as I am. Scotland, perhaps. From the shores of The Burren in Ireland, maybe. I'm as much turned on by his genteel candor as I am his graciousness. Of course, this girl is mine to claim, and he has become an unwitting competitor.

"Blimey, mate!" the girl screeches upon recognition of 350 English pounds bestowed upon her.

"If ye be her guardian, ye be doing a miserable job," the young Celt says to me, arching his eyebrow up and down in such fashion as to let me know this is merely a jibe.

"Bless you, my lord," I say to him, feeling a pang of nausea at such servility. It reminds me of the many times Dracula would dangle bawling, screeching nutriment above my head. Tatiana and Danica's as well, demanding we ingratiate ourselves, before he would feed us what the wolves brought to the glacial ingresses of the castle. I loved our husband and hated him, just the same.

"Are you with her?" the Celtic male, obviously bred of nobility, asks me with all the earnestness of a barrister beneath the glow of Parliament.

"We've only just met," I say, making sure both catch the concentration of my aquamarine eyes. Keeping the advancing crimson flare at bay.

"Me name is Corrina," the little girl says, nearly in tears at her change of luck. A part of me feels intensely awful for my own intentions. "I can't thank you enough, good sir. I've been—"

"Your reaction is ten times the frivolity I just had down on Bishopsgate, young lass," he interjects, betraying a mistiness upon his façade. He has played the role of hero, and I am evil incarnate for what I will do henceforth. "Be well, my dear, and don't spend it all in one spot, right?"

"Your generosity precedes you," I prompt the young master, who has already departed us, besotted more on Corrina's appreciation than whatever he's debauched himself with, this early part of the long evening.

"I don't recognize your money," Corrina tells me, clutching that guinea mark like she'll fight Hell to its most arcane provinces against anyone who dares try to rob her of it. "Not that I'm unappreciative."

"It doesn't spend here until I trade it at Lloyds," I tell Corrina, knowing a 100 dinar equates to nearly a guinea. Knowing also I needn't push the point much further, since the mere mention of the local bank tells her I may be from another country, but I've figured out how London commerce works. I'm as local as she needs me to be.

"I've never had this kind of—" Corrina blurts in a panic, prompting me to lean in further and clam her up before she lets all the thieves in Clerkenwell know she's ripe for the picking.

I've now decided, and it's not the money, since I've brought plenty of my own, reclaimed from the larcenous claws of Dracula, this is not just my future. This is not merely a babe to suckle on and destroy, as we did so many unspeakable times in grim and horrid Transylvania.

Corrina is my —

My daughter to-be.

"I know, young one, I know," I utter, trying to sound munificent when all I want to do is take this child into my rented room, where no questions have yet arisen why I only come out at night, and turn her. To be with me forever. "With what you've been through, such newfound fortune is no doubt overwhelming."

All Corrina does is nod down at the snow-strewn sludge and the mangled cloth doing a horrible job covering her darkened toes.

I should worry about grout or gangrene. To drink this unfortunate child's blood in this ill state is poorly-advised, yet I'm drawn to Corrina.

"I have a room with a fireplace only one block from here," I mention to Corrina, skipping the fact I haven't used a fireplace since Loznica, before my parents lost their daughter forever. "Heat to warm yourself. I can see you're so very unhappy, and not only from losing your parents. I lost mine too, you know?"

"You speak true, mum?" she whispers, still gripping that guinea like it's her very essence.

"I do, indeed, child."

I begin to feel foul from my manipulations, if only for a moment.

"And how do I know you're not out to steal me guinea?"

So young, so skeptical, so —

I shouldn't show her the true extract of my red eyes and yet I know it will soon be inevitable.

"I have my own wealth, Corrina," I say with all the confidence needed to push past her dwindling fortifications. "The guinea is all yours. I merely offer you a respite from your troubles, girl. I should warn you, however, Corrina, the money you've just come into — I'm not the one you need shield yourself against. Not in this den of cutthroats, but I *can* protect you and your guinea, my dear."

I needn't say more. By night's end, the child is mine.

The age of Queen Victoria has seen metropolitan growth unlike anything I ever expected to bear witness to, living in those garish catacombs. Yet in my eight months' time here in London, the city's populace continues to grow, especially with the influx of Irish relocating from the famine which has devastated their country. I've known hunger intimately and what it can do to someone.

Ava is one such refugee from the ravaged town of Cork. Like Corrina, Ava lost her parents to malady, her father from tuberculosis, her mother from pneumonia. Like Corrina, forced to scrape on the streets and hopping one rail system after another, until she landed at Kings Crossing, where we'd found her. Age thirteen, a shock of scarlet to her gorgeous, undulating hair, yet carrying a façade so sullen, so beyond her years, she could dexterously pass as marriage ready.

Ava didn't even put up a fight, she'd been that shattered. Other than a wince from the twin punctures I gave upon her supple neck, Ava surrendered to me and her new sister. "I know what you are and what I am now," she'd said, before passing out from her transformation.

Heba came to be one of us shortly after Ava, a nineteen-year-old girl of Egyptian descent who'd been following our new family at night. On her own, seeking work instead of matrimony in England and finding neither. Another without parents, she'd been skirting on her small inheritance from a father who'd been killed on a British archeological dig beneath the ruins of a temple dedicated to the falcon sun god, Horus. Heba's stealth had been utterly impressive as to avoid my detection, but she'd emerged from obscurity to watch us feed upon a straggling sub-lieutenant in Her Majesty's Naval Service.

By the end of that affair, Heba became a part of our dark family, all but begging for the bite of immortality. Given the ankh amulet around her olive-skinned neck, I'd nearly cringed as I would from a Christian crucifix. Yet I found the ankh, Egyptian sacred symbol for eternal life, had no repulsion effects. A kindred synchronicity, the ankh and our kind, Heba told us before leaning in to be taken. She'd tasted exquisite.

"Come now, my loves, it's time," I beckon the girls with dusk at its fullest, a new night for nourishment. We've afforded our own accommodation, a rowhome in the east end parish of Bethnal Green. It's not just lifeblood we steal in order to survive.

We've been smart to space our feedings, since word on the streets all over London is a mad slasher has been sighted in Whitechapel, a section we avoid, more out of pragmatism than due to its unappealing impoverishment.

"Yes, mum," Corrina answers with a yawn from a long day's sleep.

"I sharpened the stake before turning in this morning," Heba boasts with a haughty lift of her breasts smuggled into her bustier. Her ankh jiggles between her magnificent cleavage, which has lured many of the hapless men we've supped on. Heba lifts the cylindrical slab of wood with its dagger-like tip above her head for all of us to see. She looks warrior-proud, like her lion goddess, Sekhmet. It is me who is proud. Humbled, no less.

"This Jack the Ripper lout has taken the heat off us considerably," Ava says, sounding as refined and mature as her new older sister. "At least we dispose of our victims in proper fashion."

"Aywa!" Heba affirms in her native Arabic with a startling yowl. Of the four of us, it is Heba who has embraced vampirism with the deepest conviction, and she has greater reason. "Each Englishman in retaliation for my father!"

The Victoria and Albert Museum is where we spot an aristocratic buck tapping the cobblestones with a cane he hardly needs, carrying a swagger to his instep and a masculine crash to his hips. Even clad inside a bulky, velvet topcoat, I find enchantment by the man's strut. I find myself wanting him inside of me before I get inside *him*. I have a family, however, two girls beneath acceptable bedding age. Juvenile shells they will carry with them in their undead years to come. I was twenty-seven on the day of my rebirth when Dracula transformed me. I look no different now.

"Him, mum?" Corrina whispers with a post-winter wisp covering her voice from our intended feast.

"Aye," Ava shoves through her Irish harp. "A shame we must always take these men while in their prime."

Heba says nothing. She seeks my eye and simply nods in lieu of my consent. I can see Heba taking over our little band one day. Should we turn any other women to our fold, Heba will no doubt assert her ingrained alpha far more than her outward omega.

I give Heba the confirmation she's waiting for, and I feel a minute sense of shame when she spreads her mouth apart for me to see her ruthless amusement at the prospect of killing and drinking. Not once in my 127 years in this world, have I taken sheer pleasure in the act of murder.

Only the blood satisfies. As sex once did. With Dracula. And with Tatiana and Danica, whom I linger upon in steaming reverie for the merest of seconds, since my daughters have already begun their pursuit under the alabaster shadows of our Mother Queen and Prince Albert's emporium of the arts. Heba may enjoy the kill, but I long for something more carnal.

It is Heba who has taken the aristocrat down, but it is I, as mother of the coven, who claims first dibs. Spreading my skirts out, I straddle the poor wretch above his pelvis and despite how this may look to the girls, I can't help but grind myself against his manhood.

Alas, it doesn't respond, given his terror. Whichever frightens him more, the sight of my incisors or Heba standing ready with the sharpened end of the stake in position when we're done feeding, I cannot tell.

"A shame, just as you say, Ava," I sigh, kissing the aristocrat gently upon his wet, slobbery lips. His scream falls upon deaf ears, as his sanguinary flush coats the entire inside of my mouth. The heat of it sends an unexpected shudder into my womanhood, a faint climax I haven't felt since—

Him.

Backdoor Breaker

There's a haze smoldering over the third base side of TerraComm Park. Wonky, since it's nowhere else to be found inside the ballpark. It's a distinct vapor spewing down the shelled overhang in Sections 110 and 112 and into the visiting Detroit Wolverines' boundary of the stadium. A garrison of spectators wearing more of the opposition's gear than the home team on that side, hardly seem fazed by the ethereal phenomenon. Oblivious, more like it.

The first thought of San Diego Condors first baseman Jake Puzzella from his vantage across the diamond, is someone's flagrantly disobeying the stadium's no smoking policy by toking some high-grade grass he wouldn't mind getting a hit from himself. He's about to become a dad, though, and that carefree party boy from only a few years ago, feels like a discarded friend these days. Also, penalizations for violating the league's substance abuse policies are more than enough of a deterrent.

This cascading filter is not from the usual rolling choke of greasy onions, nachos, fries, pizza, and salsa burgers trundling onto the field from the concession stands. Nor from Brad's BBQ Bonanza, flaring its famous chipotle rub to those within vicinity of its kiosk, where dinger chasers lurk in the right field standing-room-only section, dubbed McCann Square. This is more like one of the second level concession stand cooks fell asleep and torched his kitchen altogether.

The uncanny murk manifesting out-of-nowhere on an 87-degree Monday sundown, with clear skies and the stadium more than half full on a weeknight; it's something altogether different. If the emissions were from weed, they'd filter upwards and evaporate, not ebb in a trickle-down effect, like this smoky secretion is doing.

Concentrating over the visitor's dugout, no less. Yet nobody across the diamond seems to be reacting to the mist, much less doing anything about it.

Jake's bewildered, much as he needs to keep his head in the game in the top of the sixth inning.

"I must be seeing things," he murmurs, feeling like a horror movie cliché in high socks.

From where Jake Puzzella is holding his man at first base in anticipation of a check throw from middle reliever, Juan Ladino, the ether is hard to miss. Ladino, who is carrying a stingy 1.67 ERA in his twelfth appearance a week before the All-Star break, could care less about what's going on to his right.

Not that Ladino sees it, Jake observes. None of his teammates do. They're dialed in, hunkered in position. Like he should be.

The righty Ladino has one out posted against the Detroit Wolverines, who have been clinging to a 3-2 lead going into the top of the sixth inning. Giving up a leadoff single to the Wolverines' Trey Harig, a .208 hitter who just picked up his first base hit in a week, Ladino got the next batter, Corey Salmond (a much harder hitter to send back to the bench) to jack a shallow fly which plopped harmlessly into left fielder Damon Sharpe's leather. An F7 mark for those who still meticulously keep track and scribble the scorekeeping in the stands. Salmond had also flubbed a bunt attempt trickling foul up the first base line, a dink gobbled by the fleet-footed, non-orthodox Jewish bat boy who still goes by his religious name, Avi.

Jake heard Corey Salmond's grunt of disgust at home plate and the poor display of sportsmanship by spiking his bat into the turf. The home fans had laughed as much as cheered.

How the hell does nobody else see that? Jake pleas in silence, since he's already drawn a few curious gazes from Trey Harig.

"Whattya see over there, 28?" Harig quips, getting a hefty crouch from first while keeping a firm toe of his left Adidas Adizero Afterburn planted to the white rubber sack. "You signal stealing or something? Come on, man. You guys have a better rep than this."

The query catches Jake off-guard, as if he's not already edgy from the third base dugout fog.

It's there. He knows it.

It's there! he screeches silently. *What the flying fuck is wrong with the rest of you?*

Not one of them, visitor nor home fans, appear to be unsettled, nor giving any energy to a scene as bizarre as the nest of bees the Baltimore Bombers had to contain and relocate from the 333-foot mark at the left field wall in Geppi Stadium. That game had been stopped momentarily to deal with the infestation.

Not so much as a peep here at TerraComm Park from third base umpire, Harry Wetzel, whose judgment of check swings is almost always on the dime. If he hasn't spotted the mist, then it must not be there.

And yet it is.

"No, Harig," Jake returns in a sour tone, much as he probably sounded to his teammates in Game Two against Cleveland after losing 6-to-5 in eleven innings on a squib single bringing in a walk-off for the rebranded Crusaders. The current automatic baserunner at second rule in extras has never sat well with Jake, and he doubts he'll ever make peace with it. A cheat is a cheat, even if it's league sanctioned and benefits both teams.

Juan Ladino's checking over his shoulder, as Trey Harig has now stepped off first base and is getting a little more daring with his lead. Jake closes in on the bag, expecting a check throw from Ladino, but it never comes. Instead, Ladino glances back at catcher Vito Puccio, a New York name if there ever was one, despite playing far from the Big Apple on the opposite end of the country in San Diego.

With a 1-2 count dropped upon Detroit's clean-up slugger, Bryce Reed, Jake doesn't need to see the flash of two forefingers, a single snap of the middle and fourth fingers, followed by the wiggle of Puccio's forefinger to know a breaking ball's coming.

I hope he chokes.

"What the hell—" Jake winces from an ear-puncturing voice he knows doesn't belong to Trey Harig, nor his base coach, Otis Beck, whose approachable bantering and bear-like guffawing through the prior five innings, amused Jake. Particularly Beck's self-ingratiating quip to Jake about being grateful for a night game since Detroit's bats had been sleeping all day in Sunday's 8-1 loss to the Boston Beacons.

What Jake's just heard now, whether it's a figment of auditory imagination, or something unthinkable (like the emanation only he can see), is nevertheless somehow familiar, albeit throatier, gurgling, like someone who's just had their—

"No way," Jake squeezes from lips having no interest in completing that thought. Afraid to do so. A feeling of dread worse than the time at seventeen going on eighteen when he had to come clean to his parents for sneaking out of the house with the keys to their Audi, to show off at

Lenny Bodecker's senior class party a week before graduation.

That's right, jerkoff. It's who you think it is.

Now Jake is locked in momentary paralysis. He's half praying Ladino doesn't throw a check his way, since neither of Jake's arms want to lift. Yet they must, because he needs to finish the game, and he needs to make absolute certain he isn't going off the rails from what his senses are telling him. Never mind the manifestation of a phantasm voice he's certain is talking to Jake and only Jake.

The third base smog is one thing, the voice another. Jake Puzzella, all but shits his Condors pants at what he sees down the first base line.

He sees the waved grooves of the wooden handle. He knows it well. The tip of the knife blade is also familiar to Jake and pointing at him, splashed crimson like an indictment.

You got a payback coming to ya, killer.

"It can't be," Jake eeks, loud as he dares.

Fuckin' A right it can, Puzzella. This is three years overdue.

As fast as Jake saw the knife, one he thought had disappeared in the bottom of a Michigan lake, it's no longer there indicting him on the base line.

There's an unnerving hush in the stadium, making the Mexican Hat Dance on the organ with those stupid electro taps, sound more embarrassing than usual. Even the trusty whip of acoustic frolic and snare clattering from the Violent Femmes' "Blister in the Sun," designed to prompt the fans into a quick round rally clap, fell flat by Jake's estimation, during the Condors' turn at-bat in the second inning. Queefed and rejected like The Wave from when he was a kid, which nobody does anymore.

Juan Ladino, center fielder Cesar Juarez, and San Diego's fifth man in the starting rotation, Gabriel Salazar, have been vocal about purging the Mexican Hat Dance from play at World League Baseball stadiums across the board. An age of *woke* also calling for an end to the irksome Latin march preceding a "Charge" summons from longtime organist Benny Smekal, now in his thirty-eigth year with the organization, playing that damn ditty no one's called racist until now. The octogenarian key player does peel off a mean organ version of Led Zeppelin's "Stairway to Heaven," which never grows old with the fans.

Hard to take any of it in stride with what's going on in Jake's world from first base. Jake sees most of the third base spectators have their eyes where they should be; those not plugged into their cell phones, beer cups or facing one another in conversation, anyway. Not a single finger point, a slackened jaw nor a look matching Jake's own creeped-out facade.

"Christ," he lets slip out of his mouth a bit louder this time and again Trey Harig examines Jake with scrutiny as if he's collecting intel, since Jake cannot keep his stare away from the Wolverines' dugout. Harig has no clue how Jake's legs are quaking along with his guts. A spiking case of the frets, the fearfulness.

The guilt.

The breaking ball wins this round for Ladino who pumps his fist at his left hip. Around the stadium, a digital "K" flashes across the scoreboard and around the upper deck perimeter, with the announcement Ladino has hurled his third strikeout of the game at a swift ninety-six miles an hour. Even better, the pitch count shows Ladino's only on his thirteenth in his second inning of relief work. Pitching mileage counts for everything these days, especially during contract negotiations.

Jake knows, having spent three seasons with the guy, Juan Ladino's good enough to get San Diego into the ninth inning. This in the hopes the Condors, four games behind their rival Los Angeles Griffiths for the early division lead, gets a lead of their own for their closer, Josh Reinheimer to have a crack at his sixteenth save for the year. The Condors have gnawed through a lot of close games already during the first half of the season.

None of it matters right now, not even the strikeout, as Jake frantically scans the third base side, swiveling his head and only his head, along the right field sections, until his neck strains and he eases the instant crick by skimming the crowd, up and down the rows back to home plate.

Don't worry about finding me, Puzzella. I'll find you, that's a promise.

The Condors fans finally muster up some gusto, rewarding Juan Ladino's stoic effort to keep the score from getting out of hand, responding with appreciative shouts, whistles and foot stomps. The P.A. adds to the instant party by blasting a thread of Mark Morrison's hip hop standard, "Return of the Mack."

Not a soul impacted, however, by what Jake sees, as the baseball travels around the horn from catcher, to third, to second, and snapping snugly into his own glove. He focuses just long enough to see the toss come his way. The crowd's more into Morrison's jam as people get out of their seats and grind like they just don't care, high-fiving one another and gyrating, until the next batter for Detroit shambles up to the plate.

That fog, Jesus H. Christ and all the J-man's disciples. That insane fog.

Nowhere near as insane as who Jake is hearing, whose identity has become apparent to him, and he's scared to fucking death.

"Why don't any of you see it?" Jake mumbles nonetheless, answering himself in taciturnity. Nobody *can* see it. Nobody in the whole stadium shaking ass to "Return of the Mack" can see it. Not even the drunks in McCann

Square, who make life hell on outfielders and themselves, no matter what score.

That's right, Puzzella, they can't. This is just between you and me, murderer.

Jake's mouth creaks open since he's being confronted by the metaphysical, which he's never really believed in until this very minute. It's *real*, though, by God, and apparently God seems interested in righting an old wrong.

"Glad we don't see you guys too much," Trey Harig utters to Jake, leaning without taking his left cleat off the bag. Jake's momentarily relieved for the interruption, especially since Harig's no longer eyeballing Jake as a cheater. Instead, he drops some refreshing comical griping by telling Jake, "Your boy has one of the filthiest cutters I've ever seen. Interleague can suck it."

"Truth," Jake responds with a dry smirk only for show as Harig inches back to receive some murmured instruction from Otis Beck. No doubt telling Harig to take off like his glutes are on fire upon any contact from the next batter, Cristoph Camiolo. Detroit picked Camiolo up a month ago from the Ontario Juncos in exchange for three minor league prospects and he's paid off in a hurry. The dangerous Camiolo's hitting .306 on the season and is responsible for the Wolverines' three runs with his 482-foot smashed tater back in the third inning.

Glancing down the opposite end of the diamond, the brume over the Wolverines' dugout is milkier now. Like the pea soup excretions announcing water zombie adulterers Ted Danson and Gaylen Ross who get their squishy, drowned rat revenge upon Leslie Nielsen in *Creepshow.*

Likewise, Jake's feeling neck-buried, trying to hold his breath and establish a sense of calm at the vision and a strait of something meant only for him. TerraComm Park suddenly feels just as solitary as that eerie beach of death.

Jake sees third baseman Chino Igartua and shortstop Ty Wells drop back and work a shift, which second baseman Marc Strand picks up on and follows suit. Scared or not, Jake is being paid a healthy $11.8 million a season and he has a job to do. Jake pulls from his close quarters near Trey Harig, knowing by highlights on WLB Network more than from seeing him play firsthand on a regular basis, Christoph Camiolo feeds on doubles. Many of them blasted into right field between stymied first and second basemen.

The crowd is starting to pick things up now, hoping San Diego escapes the sixth unscathed on the scoreboard.

Since Camiolo is taking his good ol' time practice swinging, scuffing his wedges in the dirt, and honking on his crotch to keep his cup where he wants it, Jake has just enough time to take a second glance at the Detroit Wolverines' dugout.

Wish we'd had Cam on our team when I was still playing, the voice burbles inside Jake's head. Like Ted Danson and Gaylen Ross, only they were choking on salty brine and seaweed. In this case, Jake knows without seeing it, like he did on the back-and-gone knife he'd used himself once, it's blood. *Of course, my career got cut short, no thanks to you, Puzzella.*

"Go die for good this time," Jake mutters with a fair distance between himself, Trey Harig, and Otis Beck, neither of whom are looking his way.

They're now checking third base side and for a glimmer of hope, Jake thinks they've finally been able to detect the garish cloud over their dugout. It's a fleeting wish.

Jake can see Wolverines manager, Rusty Ledbetter, glide his right hand down his left arm, then pat each of his flabby pectorals, before pinching his nostrils quickly, like banishing a boogie before being caught by one of the TV cameras always on the hunt for such lampoon-worthy shenanigans. Ledbetter tugs on his Wolverines ballcap, the brim going down, then to the right before settling back in its customary position.

No sign the grizzled skipper who's been in the majors long enough to say he played with the mighty Mack McGrew sees the spillage of ether into his Tiger camp.

Ledbetter's gonna win it all this year, the voice glubs again. *Starting with a sweep of you punks. Take it to the bank, Puzzella.*

"Fuck off, Darrah," Jake snaps, much louder this time, since he's resigned himself to acknowledging who—or what—the voice belongs to. A voice more prominent to Jake's past than the Detroit Wolverines, who have moved on, as all things must after their proper pauses for grief. Homicide inflicted upon one of their own if the facts be known. "There's no way you could've lived."

Take it to the bank.

"What's with you, 28?" Trey Harig scoffs loud enough to draw Otis Beck's concern and Ladino's fiery check stare before the former turns back and starts his left knee cocking wind-up.

Whatever Ledbetter's signaling to first doesn't matter, because Jake hears the whump of smacked canvas behind home plate followed by the animalistic "Ahh-rrroooo!" and a two-finger snap to the side from umpire Reggie Fowler, calling strike one on Cristoph Camiolo. Camiolo gives Fowler a sarcastic, WTF-esque look anyone in the stadium or watching on television at home would have to concede. Juan Ladino threw a ninety-seven-speed fastball that elevated inside on Camiolo. Not even a big galoot homer king like Aaron Accardo would swing at that one.

Jake's missed it altogether, because he's now surveying the home side of the stadium in search of Cecil Darrah. He can see the beer, snack, and hot dog vendors worming their way through the aisles, in their short sleeve yellow-brown button downs and, in most cases, ball caps in support of the home team. Jake can hear one of them in Section 111, directly across from the visitor's side and above San Diego's dugout wail, "Beer Man! Beer Man! Beer Man! Beeeeeeer Man!"

As irresponsible as it sounds inside his head, no matter how much distance he's put himself from the party boy days, Jake wants one of those overpriced craft IPAs right now. A hit of Jameson before that. A full cat scan of his frontal lobe before any of it.

Jake's teammates and coaches are clapping for Ladino as the new twenty-second pitch clock rule forces him to retreat from the imploring stare he shoots toward Jake. Ladino looks exasperated as he shakes his head quickly in refutation at two calls from Vito Puccio before the reliever, looking a bit antsier than he should, issues a faint nod of approval.

"Look alive, first base!" Jake hears from San Diego's seventh season head coach, Gary Nance. It might as well be smack next to his ear canal, even with the rising din of the crowd.

None of it suppresses the squishy voice nagging inside both of Jake's ears.

I'm coming for you, Puzzella.

If the veins inside his arms, very much ready to react now, could pulse any harder in reaction to the dash of his terrified heartbeat, Jake might worry about cardiac arrest. Even at the still pristine age of twenty-seven.

Win or lose, Jake Puzzella wants the hell off this field right now.

The pitch from Juan Ladino sizzles but fades right enough, prompting Puccio to snap his Wilson A2000 catching glove from his midsection and gobble it, thwarting Trey Harig a free pass to second.

Now the fog at the visitors' dugout, which gave Jake a mere case of the willies in comparison to this dire threat from a ghost of his own making, is gone, save for a few wispy tendrils. Those remind him of the filmy residue from Fourth of July fireworks his hometown Jaycees in Kennebunk throw every year.

It would've been comforting, yet what Jake sees now inside the Wolverines dugout, nearly makes him load his own cup protector with his piss.

Despite the disgusting, impossible sight of it, the first thing coming to Jake's mind is the ribald phrase, 'meatbag.' Since what he sees, and nobody else inside TerraComm Park does, is a mushroom-colored zombie inside a Detroit Wolverines uniform, looking like it's been torn in spots and dirt-clogged from the left hip and the chest. It's grubbier than a Little Leaguer's outfit never making it to the laundry hamper all summer long.

The skin beneath the filthy mesh is arcane and inscrutable, and Jake remembers having steamed crabs last season on the team's trip out to Baltimore against those same bee-infested Bombers. The locals called the ca-ca yellowish-brown ook beneath the crab's shell, its mustard. Some people ate it up, *gross,* while others shucked it aside with the crab gills, aka 'the devil' as those Old Bay spice-loving Marylanders called it. It only took hearing someone in the crab house call the ca-ca brown ook called 'crab shit,' for Jake to become a fellow shucker.

That color, that ca-ca ook inside the crab guts—the crab shit—it's what Jake sees from a decomposing once-human scowling at him from the Detroit dugout.

Jake is more than distracted; he's about to scream louder and even more unmanlier than that doofy, bushy-faced burglar in the first two *Home Alone* movies. Fortunately for Jake, Ladino's third pitch to Christoph Camiolo, is a smart sinker, baiting the Wolverines crusher for a massive whiff. Had his clubbing swing been true,

Camiolo likely would've had himself a second dinger of the game.

Now the crowd's risen to the occasion. There's cheering, clapping, a chanting of Juan Ladino's last name. The fourth pitch comes in hot, registering around the stadium at 98. Camiolo's a bit late in his swing, and the ball fouls all the way back to the announcer's booth, four levels above home plate.

Jake misses another silent summons sent his way from Ladino as he instead dares another look over the third base side, hoping the undead Cecil Darrah, the meatbag, isn't there anymore. Hope is often the biggest turncoat.

Meatbag, huh? the voice taunts him, now with a visible presence to add to the fright of it. *Hell, given what you did to me, Puzzella, I'll take it. Meatbag, that's rich!*

Jake Puzzella now wants to shuck his glove faster than crab shit, right there at the dirt cutoff of the infield and run like hell.

That thing in the Wolverines dugout, that *meatbag,* is, beyond all doubt, there for him. The gash across the throat says so. The one Jake Puzzella, the Condors' second round draft pick from eight years ago, himself put there. Even this far, the wound looks fresh, grisly, moist, pooling at the neckline of Darrah's sullied uniform. Red rivulets gush with Darrah's next incitement:

Run, Puzzella, but if you do, I'll hunt your ass down. I'll also take Hailey and your unborn on a hell ride they'll never come back from.

"C'mon, Juan!" Jake hears from the home side of TerraComm Park as Ladino inhales like he has the weight of the world on his shoulders. One would think the playoffs had started. Or worse, a threat of being demoted all the way to double-A, was pestering his pitch selection.

Gary Nance is shouting the same, waving away his pitching coach, Stan Rivers, who points to the bullpen phone in the Condors dugout. Rivers, who won the 1989 Milt Underwood Award pitching twenty-four wins against three losses (nine of them being complete games) for the Seattle Lynx, sees something he doesn't like. Nance seems to have all the confidence in the world his team is escaping the sixth and mounting a comeback SportsCenter can't help but to nudge its recap inside the first five minutes of their hourly highlights.

Back in the Wolverines dugout, the meatbag, Cecil Dannah, is skulking his way behind very much alive players, who have no notice of him. Darrah disappears only long enough between broad shoulders and a lot of hooting in support of their batter. The ghoulish façade with his slit throat glares accusatorily at Jake, until emerging on the opposite end of the dugout with a bat in his hand.

Is it bat?

Louisville Slugger becomes a curved Schrade Mach I machete inside Cecil Darrah's decomposed hand.

You like horror stories, huh? Cecil badgers Jake, wagging the glistening steel back and forth in taunt, like an oversized metronome. *How's it feel to* be *in one, chump?*

The pitch count is yet again about to expire. Vito Puccio calls time and leaps out of the box, trotting over to the mound before the Condors pitcher is charged an automatic ball for taking too long to throw under the new, hurry-shit-up WLB rules. It's something Puccio bitches as much about as Jake does, the automatic second runner rule in extra innings.

All the infielders except for Jake, have huddled around Juan Ladino with their gloves covering their mouths, to counter any possible spying. Jake feels his guts churning, punching, like the worst case of food poisoning a human could endure without dying from it.

Darrah is swinging his machete with two hands now, just like he would've in life on a baseball field, over and over behind Detroit center fielder Erik Redmon in the visitors' on-deck circle. The look in Redmon's pissy expression (one thoroughly ignorant of Darrah's presence) says he's bracing for the likelihood of not getting his at-bat this inning.

The brutal snarl to Cecil Darrah's wan face says something else altogether: revenge.

The meeting at the mound is busted up by Reggie Fowler, pushing his roly-poly umpire's chest protector into the chat, after a precursory lead time. The entire choreography has become a predictable give-and-take cycle in the time-is-money modern age of baseball. Anyone but a purist finds the game sluggish and boring. A purist enjoys the snot out of the chess match dimension to it all.

Cecil Darrah continues to swing, never taking his sunken, brackish eyes off Jake. From this distance it's hard to tell if there are any pupils inside those seemingly hollow eye sockets.

If anything, Jake should be running for his life, seven-year contract or no. He knows why Darrah is here, even if that's not really Darrah. Well, it is, but as Cecil seems to glide closer to Erik Redmon on-deck, each of those menacing swings would indicate an impending decapitation. Instead, Darrah's oscillations are lacing through Redmon instead of making contact.

In fact, Darrah pauses one of his swipes, now pointing his transparent machete directly toward Jake. Any other time in the real world, it would be a brash batter calling his pending home run shot.

"Fuck me," Jake mutters as his bowels give more of a threat than his urine.

Now Jake is hearing his manager screaming at him, not Juan Ladino. Jake catches Ladino this time, who is shooting Jake a frantic glare stating in silence, *What's your malfunction over there, Puzzella? Can't you see I have enough pressure on me?*

Ladino grimaces at Jake, as the crowd picks up a booming rhythm of support, egging him to deliver the inning-ending third strike. Trey Harig, sensing the momentary discord and Jake being slightly out of position, thanks to the hot bat of Christoph Camiolo, gets his balls up. Ladino gives him the edge because he must. Before turning his head to home plate, Ladino gnashes his teeth at Jake.

Ladino and Vito Puccio get on the same page. Only they know the cutter Harig was chawing about earlier is about to come, like the entire pennant is on the line with this single pitch.

None of them know Jake Puzzella, a Rookie of the Year nominee who fell short by two votes from the Baseball Writers' Association of America, including chairman James Crusinberry, killed Cecil Darrah and stole his wife, Hailey.

Hailey, now simmering a seven-month bun inside her womanly oven, is watching the game from the frill of a club level Skybox overlooking first base. A direct view of her man in action. Most days, Jake takes comfort when she's there at the games.

It's Hailey whom Jake is thinking about, no, *worrying* about suddenly, as her deceased, no, *murdered*, ex-husband, Cecil Darrah, has come calling for reprisal in the middle of a goddamn baseball game. Against the Detroit Wolverines, who are mincing to stay at .500 in their own record column and showing no give, in this first of three weeknight matches. Jake wonders if Hailey, no doubt chewing on pigs in blanket hors d'oeuvres in the Skybox, as a guest of the team consisting of other players' wives, can see Cecil's emergence. She'd no doubt throw up quicker than she did after the first month of conception of Jake's child.

The San Diego faithful erupt in the rowdiest manner they have all night.

Ladino again punches the air, as Christoph Camiolo smashes his bat apart over his upraised leg in anger. The Wolverines have lost their past five games and have no wish to keep their drain of drone going.

"Man, where's your head at?" Trey Harig sends to Jake, as he canters away to the circumvention of Matchbox 20 around the stadium and a flash segment on the outfield jumbotron, saluting San Diego Condors players giving back to the city's disabled children. First and foremost, Juan Ladino hugging a clean-shaven Hispanic girl, who seems to worship his utter presence.

"The hell, *tío*?" Ladino snaps at Jake, with his back to the sweetness and effervescence he's due above center field. The Spanish word *tío* in this case dropped in the vernacular of a dude or bro, instead of an uncle. Also, in said case, coming with Spanish smarm. "You look a million miles away, like you're playing for *them*. I was signaling pickoff to you while Harig was swinging his dick around, and you missed it! What's with you, Puzzella?"

Jake takes the tongue lashing but doesn't look at, nor acknowledge Juan Ladino.

It doesn't get much better inside the Condors dugout for Jake, while Rob Thomas seems to goad Jake and only Jake in song, by nattering how he's a little bit angry and this ain't over, no, not here. Thomas, and Cecil Darrah by attrition, want to push Jake around. And they will. Yes, they will.

So will Gary Nance, whose Red Man chew smells worse than uncleaned pussy, and it's all in Jake's face right now.

"I'll bench your fucking ass I ever see that sleepy shit outta you again, Puzzella! We got hungry Triple A chomping to take your spot! You may be batting .268 right now, but you're not irreplaceable! Ladino gave you the look *I* sent him, since Harig ain't stealing, not even on a goddamn high school freshman! You're leading off and they're putting in a 3-5 reliever carrying a quadruple number ERA, so I strongly suggest you get your act together!"

All Jake wants to do right now is to snake past his enraged manager into the locker room. Forget about changing into his street gear. He'll text Hailey to meet up in the players' lot inside the parking bay and they'll bolt out of Dodge. He's not sure he'll bring up what he's seen, unless she does.

Murder is murder and Hailey was a part of it, after all.

Nobody in the press will understand Cecil Darrah was an abusive piece of garbage who did unspeakable things to Hailey, rape being the lightest of his offenses.

Nor would they understand an immediate attraction fostered by hours of conversation in a Detroit hotel bar, mutual interests, dual splintering inside Jake and Hailey's respective marital situations. Jake's former spouse, Sandy, was simply tired of the baseball life, the constant absence, the away games, which went on longer in her mind than Jake's. Their divorce had been mutual, amicable, a friendship left intact. One of the few miracles in a growing American macroclimate of annulment.

"Get the fuck out there, Puzzella!" the Condors captain barks at him. "I swear to God, we lose this one, I'm putting it square on you!"

Grabbing his pine out of its slot on the bat holder, with a corresponding engraving of "28" on the knob, Jake steps out of the dugout with a shake inside both legs. They're rubbery, reminding him of that time. Yeah, *that* time, when he'd slinked up on Cecil Darrah on his favorite running trail near Bloomfield Hills, Michigan. 5:40 am, Hailey had tipped Jake off about Cecil's morning run routine during baseball season, when the Wolverines had their home games.

The wonder to it all was Jake never being caught. In her own right, Hailey's mourning act had been the sell of a lifetime.

All because I didn't want no damn kids, the bitch conned you into taking me out.

"You delusional piece of shit," Jake mumbles so nobody, especially his own riled-up skipper, can hear him. For the first time since this nightmare started, Jake is pissed off instead of scared. "What do you think half the guys on that bench over there would say if they knew the truth about you and Hailey? If I could kill you again, I'd do it."

Come and get it, then, pretty boy.

Sure enough, as Nance told him, Detroit's subbed their starter, Dack Meredith, who had a five-strikeout game going. Now in favor of Gilbert Snell, who's tossing less than blazing practice pitches which seldom cross the plate. Not that Jake can hear them, but there are rumblings around the stadium from fans of both sides over Rusty Ledbetter's questionable choice of putting in a southpaw pitcher with a bleeding earned run average, to preserve a slim lead in the bottom of the sixth.

Jake's no longer nervous on his advance to home plate, as the P.A. announcer calls him to action. Jake surveys the stadium not out of fear, but with a resolve to be rid of Cecil Darrah once and for all, as Jake's approach theme, The Weeknd's "Pray for Me" spools for the third time of the game. The reception is a bit louder than his first two at-bats, those resulting in a strikeout and a toss-out from his weak chopper to short.

Rusty Ledbetter is clapping his hands in support of Gilbert Snell, though the rest of his body language is radiating instant regret. There's a waft of fried peppers and onions Jake knows so well in this stadium, and it gives him a dubious sense of security. That, and the thought of playing Cecil at his own game—nothing to do with baseball.

Benny Smekal threads a reel of that godforsaken Latin march on the organ before twinkling off the bonding six rally notes, which send the San Diego fans into a raucous Pavlovian frenzy: "CHARRRRRRRRGE!"

Come on, Darrah, Jake chides in suppression, still finding no sign of Cecil anywhere. *Go back to the grave where you belong. I won, motherfucker. I won.*

Gilbert Snell, who has enough of a pooch spilling over his uniform belt to have corralled fat shaming memes from online trolls, stares down Jake like he loathes him nearly as much as Cecil Darrah does.

For show, as much to his manager as himself, Number 28 takes a few lazy winds forward of his bat before settling in for the delivery by Gilbert Snell.

You think you won, eh?

The baseball sails past Jake, a lean 83-mile-an-hour curve for strike one. A mere lob in comparison to the young heat seekers of today, who likely have no clue an eighteen-season flamethrower named "Bullet Bill" Ewing ever existed.

After tossing the ball back to Snell, Detroit's catcher, Lucio Citino, pounds his fist into his oversized glove over and over, seemingly to unnerve Jake into taking the second pitch again.

"Alright, Citino, I see you," Jake cracks, taking a precursory glance down at the catcher, whose sneer behind his grilled mask has more of an effect than the glove whumping.

For a split second, Citino's face erases and becomes replaced by Cecil Darrah's lurid visage. Those hollow eye sockets are pocked with stretched sinew. The nose looks more than broken; it's mashed down and spread across specter Darrah's cheeks. Beneath the catcher's mask is an undeniable throat gash.

You won nothing, *prick.*

"Sometime today, batter," Lucio Citino, the real one, mocks with furrowed brows back at Jake.

"Step in before I give you an automatic strike two," Reggie Fowler warns Jake. His perturbed expression matches Citino's from behind his ump mask.

Jake complies, feeling his momentary insurrection retreat, foiled in a hurry, nearly as ill-advised as Pickett's charge at the battle of Gettysburg in 1863.

If Jake hadn't been shaken once again by the in-and-out manifestation of Cecil Darrah, so much he pulled his stance like something had jerked his shoulders back, Jake would've seen the intended splitter eating the dirt for ball one.

Jake can see Juan Ladino in the Condors dugout in private chat with one of the other relievers, Chris Hayes. Their guffawing at Snell's gopher ball does nothing to settle Jake.

Enough of the head games, Jake hears, as if he's still in control of Lucio Citino, who's looking more miffed now at his own pitcher. He tosses a fresh game ball to Snell passed to him by the ump.

Fowler tosses the scuffed baseball to Avi, who's so fast in his pre-adolescent work Jake almost misses hearing the kid chirp at him, "You got this, Jake!"

Lightning quick, that kid, but who cares about lightning quick kids if you're Jake Puzzella right now?

It takes everything Jake has, not to hurl his pregame peanut butter power bar all over home plate, since he's tasting it a second time from the gorge bubbling inside his throat.

"Holy shit!" Jake shrieks.

On the mound, next to Snell, is Cecil Darrah.

As if anyone else but Jake could see it happening, Cecil Darrah has conjoined his essence into Gilbert Snell's body. Possessing him, as it were. Like that replicant prostitute-insurrectionist, Mariette and Joi, the A.I. sexbot in *Blade Runner 2049* abutting as one to give Ryan Gosling's am-I-human? Agent K a shag for the dystopian ages.

Jake's not even reset in the batter's box. He does the unthinkable if you're a spectator or a baseball announcer. He hoists his bat over his shoulder with both fists, like he and Hailey did, throwing hand axes at wooden wall targets at one of those novelty meaderies on their third date, once feeling comfortable to be seen in public together. Nary a word between them about the fact Jake had opened the esophagus of Hailey's late husband, but it had been on his mind the entire time.

Only then does Jake realize he's doing what Cecil Darrah did moments ago with that bat-turned-machete. No sign of either instrument, since Darrah and pitcher Gilbert Snell are one.

Lucio Citino shouts as he springs up to intervene. "What the shit're you doing, Puzzella?"

Players swarm out of both dugouts, some aiming for Snell, some for Jake and Citino, some for one another. All of it, too late to stop the predestined.

This time, the baseball *flies*. Bugs Bunny would be nattering, *"That's givin' 'em the ol' pepper, kid!"*

It's not just a breaking ball. The ball has *broken bad*.

Despite his jolt, scream, and attempt to duck, Jake cannot escape where the scorching hurl lands: smack in the center of his head.

The last thing Jake Puzzella sees before his batting helmet cracks at the brim, soars off his head, and his world blanks, is the scoreboard showing the pitch clocked at an inhuman 128-miles-an-hour.

That October, Jake Puzzella is sitting in a motorized wheelchair, his head locked into place by a contraption so unreal, it feels more of a prison than the rest of his inactive body.

His baby daughter, Arielle, is inside his lap, though the infant is being held in place by her mother to avoid her tumbling out from Jake's forced immobilization.

Hailey hasn't smiled in weeks. In fact, she looks haggard, renounced beyond her twenty-seven years. It's hard to tell exhaustion from regret, but each ring apparent to Jake. He's heard Hailey tell her mom on the phone more than once, she feels cheated. He despises it as much as everyone telling him how lucky he is to have survived being beaned by a projectile at a velocity that would've killed him, had he not been wearing the batter's helmet.

Jake can speak, but seldom does. When he feels an urge to say anything, it's usually an apology to Hailey for his part in this entire disaster they've found themselves in. Hailey shushes him, in the attempt to be amiable, but it's already apparent she resents Jake as much as she once loved him, for rescuing her from Cecil.

On the TV, the International Series is on, a rare Game Seven between the Kyoto Tanuki (their mascot being a Japanese native racoon) and the Detroit Wolverines.

The will of bored baseball gods looking to shake up the natural order the championship should come down to this, a winner-take-all with Detroit ahead by two runs in the ninth inning. The Tanuki were predicted to run the table with ease after finishing the regular season at a spectacular 105 wins and 57 defeats. They've lost only twice through the Western Conference playoffs. Meanwhile, the Wolverines took a harder run of the gauntlet through the Eastern Conference as an 83-79 wild card, and they are being heralded by the press as upset darlings.

It was Lucio Citino's eighth inning grand slam which brought the Wolverines back from a 4-2 deficit. For all the marbles in the bottom of the ninth, it's Detroit closer, Brady Porpora, who blew seven save opportunities all season, but has now been ringing a commanding 1.02 ERA including shutout ball through four opportunities in the playoffs.

Gilbert Snell had a disastrous finish to his shortened season, earning World League Baseball's first ban since Roberto Sandovar and Mickey Grier in 2021. Worse, he's been institutionalized, since nobody believes he wasn't in control of himself when he'd ended Jake Puzzella's career, much less mobility. Hailey wants to sue Snell and has a sharp litigator named Macy Esposito on retainer. Her San Diego-based power firm, Howard, Kiel, and Brockman have already filed the civil lawsuit, but Snell's assets have been frozen as a ward of the state of California. Restitution will be long coming.

It doesn't make things any better those bloodsport-chasing internet trolls divided their anonymous snark between Snell and Jake. After all, the video clearly showed Jake making a threatening gesture toward Snell with the bat. Calls for Jake's likewise ban from the league have finally fallen silent, given his 'natural consequence,' as it's been lamented by numerous baseball commentators.

Porpora forces a groundout at second and a deep fly to at the warning track. Though the Tanuki won home field advantage through the playoffs, it's the well-traveled Wolverines fans who rule Kyoto City Stadium right now. Their enthusiasm rings of euphoria, as former cellar dwellers are about to knock out the current titans of the game. Only the Stanley Cup is harder to win.

"Good for them," Hailey says, looking at the television more than her husband, while cradling baby Arielle to her abdomen, then to her heart. Lightly cheering with her head slumped for a few of the Wolverine players she once considered friends from a different time of her turbulent life.

Porpora fulfills an apparent divine sports prophecy by drilling home a called third strike on a 91-mile changeup.

Of all the muscles left to him, Jake contracts his eyebrows and wrangles his parched lips, half longing for, and half dreading his next meal, which Hailey must spoon feed him. As mushy as what baby Arielle's been hanging with in her short time on the planet.

Worse than the ingratiation on the tube and the indignation of losing his career, is the beleaguering voice inside his head which has been there ever since anyone last saw Gilbert Snell, much less Jake Puzzella, play the game.

As I said, you won nothing, Puzzella.

Lunch Break

I knew the minute I stepped out of the office and onto the elevator, where I was going for lunch. Nowhere you would get customer service, not in the traditional sense. Nowhere you would bring your food back in a bag. Sustenance comes in other fashions, from other sources. Sometimes you just gotta be willing to break taboo.

All morning long, I let my eyes linger with expectancy upon the pounding snow outside the window from my office. Four inches overnight added to the half foot dumped onto Baltimore two days ago. According to all the local forecasts and the national Weather Now app, the entire eastern seaboard was in for another a full day of snow barrage, beyond today's projected foot.

Let the snowbirds revel and the kids blow raspberries at their schools, since the city hasn't seen a winter this relentless in years. I only like it since it keeps people off the streets, for the most part.

Most businesses shut down in inclement weather like this, or let their employees work remotely online at least, but not restaurants or grocery stores or gas stations.

Especially not a downsized mortgage brokerage starving for new applications.

The sloppy commute from home to the Metro station was a crapshoot, and the wait for a train was doubled before the slow and sluggish descent into the city.

I passed the time checking my nosediving stocks I would have to sell very soon and reading up on local politics, which are, these days, more diverting than the entertainment section of any news site. I downloaded steak and rib recipes to my phone and managed my fantasy football, baseball, and soccer leagues. We're not far off from March Madness and I'm already taking Clemson versus Xavier for all the men's collegiate marbles. Iowa versus Connecticut as usual in the ladies' brackets. I won both NCAA pools last year with North Carolina and Iowa respectively. With my winnings, I'd treated myself to a vertical meat smoker, sporting 710 square cooking inches.

Let it snow, I say, since when it snows this much and this hard, you can't ask for better cover.

"A half hour break is a half hour, Mr. Tanner," I heard to my back, refusing to turn all the way in acknowledgement of my boss, Josephina. The gritty tone to her warning felt less like an indictment and more of a realistic threat, given the crippling slowdown in the real estate market.

Also given my returning to the office later and later from lunch these days. Sometimes as long as fifteen minutes extra.

It's a wonder we were open at all, much less during such prolonged harsh weather. Connelly Mortgage Investors was just old school that way, it ringing more like the name of a funeral home. With the Fed refusing to bump interest rates down from 8.25% in a stagnant sellers' market, pushing overinflated properties (most in need of equity busting rehab), it's no wonder we were so dead.

Accordingly, I was on borrowed time.

Yet beyond the implied hit in income, I just didn't give a shit. Joblessness would be coming soon enough, but I have Clemson winning at an early-on 13-to-1 Vegas odds. It's a sure thing.

Our workforce had already been slashed by more than half, testified by the emptied, sterile partitions showing only the gutted loose phone cords and computer equipment, removed along with the people who'd manned them. Customer service reps and lead generators like Kristy Hoder, Connor Greene, Evan Bennett, and Nadia Alinsky. People I missed already, even if I took strange comfort in the diminished chaos of ringing phones and clacking keyboards. Connor and Evan had been my sports buds. Kristy and Linda, my lifeline to all things feminine with which to dazzle my grumbly housebound wife, Gidget.

"I want to go out when you return, Marc," was the next needling voice I heard. Our toady narc of a receptionist, Kelly, whose idea of going out to lunch was merely to slip down to the commissary on the second floor. There she would wet and nuke her freeze-dried instant meal of the day and dive into the latest Sophia Solomon romance epic on her Lustra digital reader. If I led a boring life, Kelly's (a cute name for the dumpiest of a thirty-one-year-old girl with no marital prospects on the horizon) was duller than a pre-licensure webinar.

"We have less staff than normal, hence lesser coverage," Josephine added, reminding me of Gidget on a cleaning bender whenever I'd leave behind a ring from my coffee mug on the porcelain kitchen tops.

Even without looking at Josephina, I could feel the pretentiousness oozing out of her. The same supercilious way she harped on her staff when the paper towels ran out of the dispenser next to the kitchen sink, or someone other than her, as the office manager, didn't take it upon themselves to order more toner once the last drum was installed into the copier. A long-discontinued Toshiba, more ancient than the wrinkles creasing Josephine depleted eyes.

As spent and pointless as Josephine's perpetual reminder every day between 11:30 and 1 pm to the handful of her remaining employees, "One of us will need to cover the phones to relieve Kelly, just a reminder."

I was hanging by a thread, but thus far I have been considered borderline indispensable, since I have a loyal pipeline of builders and developers, who normally have new build contracts spurting all over my CPU in better times.

What little I get these days, is the random drop-in from aggressive house flippers. Grab and go make-a-buckers sick of the private hard money rehab lenders who may have leaner underwriting restrictions than the traditional banks we farm to, but many of these rowhome raiders have no interest in restoration. Such bird-in-hand shade is one reason why Charm City has been steadily losing its sparkle. Do a title search on your average inner-city property; the convoluted ownership chain will make you dippy.

"Yes'm," I called back to Josephina, reining in my miasma of angst and sending her a wave of confirmation I didn't really intend to honor.

Josephina and Kelly could wait. If what I was going to do at lunchtime was quick enough as the past two times, we'd all get what we wanted from a day where the phones were colder than the frosty bluster outside.

A half hour lunch in corporate Baltimore is usually just enough to scoot across the street to Manny's Burgers and lose half the time in line with fellow starving loan officers from competing banks and title escrow attorneys scrounging for any scrap to close a deal with. None of them are willing to chat and compare notes for obvious reasons.

Considering the staff at Manny's were often part-time workers and full-time junkies, it was theoretical whether they got your order right. There was always a separate queue for frustrated customers hounding the always frazzled manager for a redo or a refund. Reminds me of the occasional mortgage borrower who takes me to the mat over a floating administration or title exam fee I have no control over.

Manny's was the only surviving fast food establishment within two blocks, given the bail outs of the woebegone Mexican, Chinese, and sushi places which used to give the brackish Charles and Baltimore Streets some sense of ethnic lilt. Even the fried fish and polish dog hucksters had packed their steamy roller carts and bailed. Baltimore City Courthouse three blocks down, used to be a happening place at noon on a summer workday.

Josephina becomes an afterthought once the elevator opens for me and only me. It takes no time to traverse sixteen floors before a chill hits me once crossing into the atrium of the main lobby.

I'd been in a good mood this morning coming into the work, despite Gidget insisting I wear the dumb yellow and orange paisley tie she gave me last Christmas, and of course, the even dumber matching socks. I love Gidget to death, but there are times I feel she and Josephina are cut from the same cloth; women who believe they have the upper hand over me, women who clock-watch and attempt to micromanage me.

Women who have the furthest clue how I tick.

Outside the Conway Building, the wintry punch everyone's been grousing about this week takes a shot at my face, reminding me I'd forgotten to pack lip balm into my briefcase, one I tote around these days more as a pose. Five months ago, it was stuffed with new loan applicants to follow up with at home after dinnertime.

Damn, I'm hungry.

Snowflakes batter my eyes, dotting them with an icy wetness I could do without. The concrete overhang in front of the building does little to shield from the runaway fragments. It's currently packed with other office workers looking as fed up as I feel. I can't understand why there are so many of us working onsite during such an ugly week of weather, though I have my own reasons for being here at work.

None of which have anything to do with work itself.

A bumblefoot maintenance guy everyone knows here as "Nicky" pushes a metal shovel along the granite slate of the patio, creating a noisome ruckus I could likewise do without. He's scooping up very little snow. More like the remaining bits of salt he'd put down this morning. Nicky's vicious cycle of futility will spin again once he trudges by to fetch the salt bucket stationed next to the second of the two rotary doors.

"You missed some there, chief," a youngblood suit says to Nicky's lack of a shadow. Nicky's as oblivious as the snow clogging the gutters and the streets, the latter getting cleared by means of privatization instead of legislative approval. This is due to the city's marginal snow removal budget being squandered after the season's first two storms a couple weeks back.

This smug punk heckling Nicky is a junior stockbroker I know, and not just because I've seen him blustering into Bragg and Henry with a head of steam to prove himself. It's more the purposeful loiter of his head. A purebred Yale-type smartass. Furthermore, it's the buck's lazy eyes and overcooked laughter at his own pathetic jibe in the company of his fellow youngbloods stuffed inside their carved, not tailored, Alexander Amosu designer suits. One of them, a mulatto-skinned kid no older than twenty-five, towers over us all. He glances down at me and shakes his head as if to say, *Don't blame me for this peckerhead's lameness.*

I call to mind that memorable diss in the original *Scream* movie, *"Hey, it's called tact, you fuck rag."*

It makes me want to kill the little greenhorn on sight, but I'm not the killing kind.

I glance at my watch but not because I'm concerned about Josephine's futile intimidation. I have a meeting in an alley and I'm a few minutes early. I've grown fond of the alley. Not because it's an alley, that's just dumb.

It's because — well, because I do things there Gidget, much less Josephina, would scream holy terror at, and have me put away if they knew.

My mouth tastes coppery right now, because I've just bitten down on my tongue and the fresh blood inside is like a treat. An appetizer, actually.

I mean it; I am freaking *hungry* right now.

The junior stockbrokers get a quick jump with almost everyone making squishy sounds enroute to Manny's Burgers, their patent leathers slopping the slush around their dress socks. Punctuation mark to an incessantly sloppy winter, protracted by that fatuous groundhog from Punxsutawney. I can't believe it's still a thing civilized people pay attention to.

I haven't eaten a conventional lunch from Manny's or otherwise, in weeks. Gidget keeps asking me where my appetite is these days, since we always have leftovers. I used to have seconds of just about anything she makes, especially anything with beef or pork in it.

"My man," I hear to my left as I slow my slippery roll before getting to Calvert Street. "You're early. Good thing I came over this way ahead of time, cold as it's been and bound to get worse. Going down to the teens later. Not that I get my news the same way you do, watching that cute, skinny white girl meteorologist from Channel 11 on a 52-inch projection tube."

"Privileged, you want to say," I mock, playing along with his roast. Truth be told, we have a moderate 37-inch Toshiba from Walmart, and our savings are close to tapped since Gidget doesn't work. I'll never say it loud, especially not to my wife, but I've been fishing from my retirement fund. If I hadn't started doing *this*, I'd have saved a bundle. Clemson, don't you dare flop on me, my dudes. A ten grand bet at 13-to-1 means everything to me right now.

I hold my fist out to the husky man I only know as Curtis, realizing I'd been in such a hurry to go to lunch I left my black Isotoner gloves on my desk. It gets tapped harder than usual by an ebony-tinted set of knuckles. I don't show any hint of pain, but it feels like Curtis put more into his dab than usual. Like he wants to drive home a point.

"As you say, boss," my friend — at least I think he's a friend after these past few months — tells me with a faint jeer wiped away by the emergence of two ironically bundled, menopausal women griping how ineffective Mint-o-Pause heat flash reducers are. In this weather, of all things to bitch about.

"Whattya got for me today, Curtis?" I ask, trying to assert myself without coming off like I no doubt sound; a pretentious, middle-aged loan officer with a lame, repetitive life seeking filthy pleasures out of plain sight. You'd think he was pimping me a whore.

There are different pleasures of the flesh to behold and seldom few who act upon it.

"I know you're usually on the clock, Mr. Tanner. Hell, I remember the days when I—"

"Don't worry about that," I cut him off, flash-checking around as Curtis pulls back into the alley he came out of. One I've grown to know in a hurry, a murky hellhole smelling of piss and rotted food. I've grown used to it. Doesn't even spoil my appetite at this point.

I don't see just yet what Curtis always has on-hand, what he motherfucking lured me in to begin with.

A hard, Styrofoam-based cooler like Omaha Steaks uses to ship meats across the country with the dry ice inside.

"What'd you get this time?" I ask ravenously, sounding like I probably did as a kid hocking my parents whenever they got back from the grocery store in the hopes they'd brought me a box of Twinkies or Cookie Crisp cereal. "Thigh meat? Shoulder?"

I may as well be at Wegmans hounding their meat manager for their choicest cuts of ribeye, my stomach is growling that much with anticipation.

"Nah," Curtis answers and I know he's baiting me. We move further into the dimmer part of the alley where nobody else is except the snow and I still can't see the cooler I'm expecting. For that matter, Curtis is usually handing me the latex gloves by now, and he shows no sign of doing that.

My hands quiver from both the cold and because they long to be sheathed in moist, scarlet meat.

"Torso this time?" I ask keenly, thinking of the 5,400 caloric value which could come my way since I've done my due diligence. With the same thoroughness as my sports picks. I never roll the bones unless it's a sure thing. "Just not another pancreas, alright? I think the last one you got me was a diabetic. Didn't feel right settling."

"Impatient as always, Mr. Tanner," Curtis says with an officialness I find off-putting, like he's the one in control instead of me, as the customer.

As if he's *always* been in control.

"Where is it, Curtis?" I blurt, feeling panic rising inside of me. I look over my shoulder again in the unlikely event I've been followed, especially by a cop. To think there was a time in American history when this sort of thing was legal.

Nothing there but the flutter of drifting snow.

"Where's the damn cooler?" I come at Curtis more forcefully, as if I have the right. As a paying customer, though, I kinda do. "I have your money in my pocket, though I'm going to have sell some of my portfolio at a loss and keep drawing from my 401K if I keep doing this. The early withdrawal fees are killing me."

"I'm afraid I have nothing for you today," Curtis blurts, a twin blast of vapor pouring from his nose and out the corner of his mouth. His frayed clothes make him look dangerous now, instead of destitute. I would say Curtis sounds perturbed, but that's not it. It's something far more alarming to me. This time, I'm feeling nervous being here, the snow covering our heads and our shoulders, if not our latest proposed transaction.

Still, I want it in my mouth.

It's going to break me, maybe be the death of me because I'm hooked, and I want it. I *want* it!!!

God, what's *wrong* with me?

I want the meat. I'd grill it at home if I could convince Gidget it was a monster section flank steak I'd bought at Costco, which I foresee us having to drop soon, even if they're far cheaper than what Curtis brings me.

Spice it with carne asada, harissa, and Montreal rubs and throw it in the smoker. Goddamn, it would be ten times better than raw.

Then again, human flesh in the raw is its own delicacy. Like certain parts of the world savor ox tail, tuna eyes, pig snouts, duck tongues, haggis, animal stomach linings called tripe, all of which I used to find disgusting. The Middle East and Eastern Europe have khash, which is stewed cows' heads and feet, where the skulls are left to grin at you while you pick them clean. I understand it all better now, especially blood pudding. Blood congeals inside raw human flesh, after all.

"Oh, I almost caught you one behind the Rusty Scupper across the harbor last night. Young fine thing, no older than nineteen. Drunk off her cute white ass, but she gave me a damn fit anyhow and got away. If not for all this snow, I probably would've been seen. Look, Mr. Tanner, if you want me to keep bringing your, ah, *lunches,* then the price goes up. Three grand from here on out."

"Three grand?!?" I exclaim, feeling both dirty and manipulated at the same time. "Are you out of your mind, Curtis? I work on damn commissions and originations are dry as shit right now… and even if they weren't… three grand?!"

"Ain't my problem, now, is it, you sick sumbitch!"

I see the flare of Curtis' nostrils and radiation inside his bloodshot eyes. Only now, do I smell the cheap gin on his breath from his pink lips curling into scorn. Gordon's 40 proof 750-milliliter bottle going for less than fifteen bucks. Cheap respite from hard times for anyone, much less than the homeless. Pure rotgut, I'd know it anywhere. I have some of the same in a flask tucked into my desk to nip on at work, along with a canister of Orbit mint gum. All part and parcel of my post-lunch coverup.

"I don't have that kind of money, goddammit!"

My stomach starts twisting into knots. My throat feels arid at first, then cooked, as a nervous chunk of bile blasts into my esophagus. Reminds me of my college drinking days when I was afraid less of the hangover and more of those obnoxious puke gorges torching my Adam's apple.

"You want me to keep up this operation, you pay me what I ask. You want to quit this little agreement we have, then hell, Mr. Tanner, it's no skin off my teeth. I got other customers."

"You conniving piece of street trash! I've been paying you eight hundred each time and now you want to price gouge me? Are you even legitimately homeless?"

"Not my problem, as I said," Curtis replies arrogantly without addressing my questions. I want to punch his silver capped teeth out for his audacity.

My real problem is I'm getting hungrier. I want to eat, *right now.*

If Gidget only knew what I've been having for lunch all this time. I'd nearly busted myself earlier in the week, telling her the reason I couldn't eat little more than half a plateful of her Italian sausage casserole. One of her go-tos. It was human calf that day, female, a co-ed from John Hopkins, so Curtis had claimed.

I'm feeling squeamish now, instead of out of my mind hungry. Something about this arrangement stinks, and not just my breath after these meals.

"Alright, Curtis," I hear a second voice come from the darkest end of the alley. "I don't need to see anything else. He's worth your asking price."

Curtis backs even further away from me, the eruptive grin on his face selling a double-cross I never saw coming. His hand goes up to nothing at first, then it's filled with a thick roll of money.

I now see Curtis for what he really is, and impoverished is the furthest thing. The man's a full-fledged player, probably laying his head on plush pillows beneath silk bedding in a swanky two-bedroom condo up in Charles Place. The Gordon's gin being as much of a coverup as my own.

I want to feel shame for what I've done, but now that I've been made prey instead of predator, I feel not so much angry, but—defeated.

I'm all but certain I'll never see Gidget ever again. Josephina and Kelly's lunch relief? Well, as Curtis himself said, not my problem.

"Eight thousand, as agreed," the new voice says. I still can't see him, but it's a man's voice. Low, concrete, terrifying. "This one's in reasonable shape for his age. You'd be amazed what needs are filled by the human organ black market, since donors are at an all-time low. Demand's always high, and I have clients who'll pay anything my company asks so they have a second chance at life."

"Thank you, my man, a pleasure doing business as always," Curtis tells the scary-pitched arrival, who now emerges, though I only see his lengthy arm pointing a gun capped by an elongated silencer at me. I know Curtis' phraseology to a tee; he's dropped the same exact spiel upon me after I've finished my lunches. "There's more where that came from."

I want to scream my betrayal at Curtis, but the muffled gunshot cuts me off.

The Grinning Soul

2011. When CDs were still a *thing*.

Evan had a problem.

It wasn't just the reek of patchouli that would cling to his suit jacket and give him away. His wife Karla would detect it quicker than the occasional cigarette he snuck behind her back.

Assuming she came home this evening.

Just last night he'd called Karla a bitch for crumbling a pack of cigarettes he'd stowed away behind his stereo in the basement. She'd gone so far as to make a show of it, through gnashed teeth in front of the twins, Jared and Isaac, boasting how she'd found the cigarettes, then mashing them in front of Evan's face before pitching the shredded muddle into the garbage.

"As much as tobacco costs these days," Evan growled, slamming the door of his silver Dodge Caliber. The four-door family vehicle, which had just come out of the shop for the third time this year (this time for a suspension problem he'd be months paying off), wobbled on its axles before settling in place.

Every time Karla caught a whiff of tobacco on Evan, she took him to the mat over it. He'd cut down from one pack of Camels a day to a few singles a week, but Karla didn't see the achievement there. She'd called Evan weak, right there in the kitchen, the pot of Italian sausage spaghetti she'd cooked upside down in the sink. The boys saw it all, looking more incredulously at their father than their mother, who'd flung their dinner in aggravation at Evan, cutting him down further by telling him his lack of discipline was pathetic.

After Evan dropped the b-bomb on her in retaliation, Karla shipped off with the boys to her mother's house, leaving the discarded spaghetti and sausages where she'd hurled it.

"I got you on the cleanup, Kar," Evan said sourly with nobody to hear him in the parking lot of The Chain Effect record store. Even with all the other cars there, Evan still had enough privacy to add, "Didn't know you had *that* in you."

Though he would never admit it to Karla, whenever she came back, he'd run out to the 7-11 convenience store immediately after pitching the sopping noodles and leftover wasted sauce into the trash can. He'd found sauce specks this morning, having missed them in in his anger the night before, dotting the plastic dish drain and along the quartz countertop. They looked to Evan like drops of dried blood.

Evan had bought two new packs of cigarettes to spite Karla and binge smoked like he had in his ephemeral days of post-college bachelorhood. Evan puffed like a demon under the stars on the far end of the deck, relishing the momentary liberation, mindlessly blowing smoke rings, and belching pretend Godzilla emissions. He'd smoked seven sticks in the span of two hours, dunking the spent butts into a paper cup filled with water and pouring the evidence down the storm drain across from the townhouse.

The longer Karla refused his calls and text messages last night, the less culpable Evan felt about stashing the remainder of the first pack of Camels plus the standby second inside his glove compartment.

"Calling you a bitch may have been out line," Evan grumbled, "but you were no better, castrating me in front of the boys. The longer you carry this standoff, I—"

Evan left that threat unfinished, not only feeling stupid for talking to himself out loud, but for letting last night get to him so much all he could think about this morning was blowing money he didn't really have on CDs instead of reconciling with Karla.

The earthy redolence of patchouli swirling inside The Chain Effect slammed customers as they walked into the music store. No doubt burned in the back of the store or even on the floor, to cover up some after-hours ganja pulling, since there were no actual incense sticks for sale.

It didn't matter Evan already owned more than 4,000 CDs and 300 slabs of vinyl. He was good for dropping anywhere from fifty to eighty bucks on tunes each trip to The Chain Effect. Calculating his wish list to the point of distraction at work, Evan knew he would easily spend that range once again.

Already twelve minutes into his lunch break, Evan double-timed his steps amongst the waist-high CD racks. His fingers flipped jewel cases forward in rapid fashion, executing swift nudging movements that would appear blurry to the casual eye. In essence, he came to The Chain Effect to relax, but relaxation had hardly been afforded him these days with an Accounts Payable job which was never a straightforward 9-to-5 schedule. Plus, a set of twin boys always in his face during most of his waking hours at home. Usually wanting him to watch, not actually game *with* them on the PlayStation.

The irony of Evan having so much music was he didn't have the time to enjoy it all, even if he'd found himself missing Jared and Isaac last night while spinning The

Allman Brothers' *Idlewood South* album inside an empty house. This after showering and sending his smoke-covered clothes through the wash.

Right now, The Clash's ska-splashed "Wrong 'em Boyo" from their seminal *London Calling* album crashed and skanked around every crevice of The Chain Effect. The morphing globs of wax amalgamating inside lit halogen lava lamps around the store conflated in a psychedelic reverie behind Scot-Brit Joe Strummer's infectious warbling.

A door poster with Elvis Presley encased inside his '68 Comeback leather devotions, held sentry on the door leading to the stock room. An enigmatic pose of The King caught in mid-shimmy and an elevated regal paw as The King of Rock 'n Roll. Some wit of the store had taped a hand-crafted word balloon behind Elvis' rawhide-hugged butt with the word *FART!!!* written upon it. Evan never failed to chuckle whenever he spotted it.

Of the employees at The Chain Effect, only the older guy barely taller than the cash register, was beyond college age. The other three appeared in the right age bracket to be attending Towson University two miles away, yet they were reliably found working the store. The thinning blond hair and the horn-rimmed glasses of the older guy, screamed geek chic, like Dana Carvey's Garth Algar finally surrendering to a haircut. His blue-and-black-checked flannel shirt was reminiscent of the days of drab when Pearl Jam ousted Poison from Billboard. At his age, though, the manger looked displaced from the paramount straight edge punk movement of the eighties birthed a fair beltway trip away in nearby Washington, DC.

Evan had a handful of CDs in his hand, most of them used, one of them new: *Summerteeth* and *Yankee Hotel Foxtrot* by Wilco, Imelda May's rockabilly romping *Mayhem*, Herbie Hancock's modish fusion ride *Thrust*, and

Yes' prog push of *Going for the One.* The latter was an album Evan had long avoided, based on complaints of uber-complexity from snooty hipsters he used to surround himself with before falling into nuclear family mode. Original Yes vocalist Jon Anderson sang on *Going for the One;* how could it lose? It couldn't wank any deeper than *Tales from Topographic Oceans,* Evan justified to himself, feeling his domestic angst wane simply being in the store.

"Are you finding everything alright, sir?"

She was the only store clerk who bothered to approach Evan whenever he came into The Chain Effect. Beyond a routine greeting as he walked in, the rest of the staff almost never checked on him.

Her ebony face mirrored the sweetness in her voice. It was framed by spidery black hair still smartly managed — a demure-punk styling, like Darryl Hannah's sprouting coif as Pris in *Blade Runner.* The effervescence of the black girl's silky cheeks, her contenting brown eyes and her warm smile, lent the young girl (Evan's junior by seventeen, eighteen years maybe, he figured) a winning combination of allure and intellect. Her neck — always craned a few inches whenever she queried Evan — was so delicate, he envisioned her either giggling or surrendering herself to a pair of lips caressing it.

"I'm good," he answered in flat monotone, though he wanted to engage her further.

Evan didn't want to hurt Karla even more than he had last night, but as he drank in the black girl's dancing eyes, he'd come to the realization he patronized The Chain Effect for her, as much as the music. Cheating on Karla had never crossed Evan's mind beyond jacking off to his Nina Hartley porn videos in the rare times he could sneak into the basement alone in the witching hour on a Friday night. Cheating wasn't on his mind right now, although it wasn't outside the realm of entertaining.

If only the staff wore name tags.

"K," the clerk responded at a near-whisper. "Let me know if I can help you find something."

The girl had a stack of vinyl albums bundled inside her arms and her purple-wrapped breasts hung over them like a provocation. Her shirt was cut daringly low. Any hetero male — attached or not — wouldn't miss that. Usually, she wore modest button-down blouses offering very little view of her upward slopes. No disguising them this time and there was plenty to behold.

Her russet-tinted cleavage called out to Evan like a safe place, or at least a confidential diversion, as she scooted toward the vinyl racks. She didn't check on any of the four other customers milling about, he noted. Two of whom, a pair of square-haired men Evan figured were a couple, given their playful hip-bumping, were having a tizzy over which Swinging London era singer of the 1960s had sung "Your Hurtin' Kinda Love," Leslie Gore or Dusty Springfield. Springfield of course being the correct answer.

Did the girl's pinpointed attention upon Evan mean anything at all?

By the time Evan was ready to check out, she was waiting for him at the register. As usual. It just now occurred to Evan he couldn't remember the last time anyone but her rang him out.

The violet-loving girl's older colleague was changing discs in the store's stereo, pitted behind the register, and within seconds David Bowie's *Hunky Dory* was pumping through the store. The other two clerks had vanished to the stock room, no doubt engaging in activity requiring a fresh patchouli dusting.

Evan recognized "Life on Mars?" within its first bar, though he wondered why the preceding three songs of the album had been skipped, including Bowie's longtime hit containing everyone's favorite rock mantra: *ch-ch-ch-ch-changes.*

"That one's for you, Patrice," Garth-with-a-Crop told her as he swung away from the register.

Patrice. Now Evan had a name. Patrice. As exquisite as the frame it was attached to.

"Thanks, Neil!" she called back to Garth-with-a-Crop, though her stare was fixated upon Evan. Her shoulders started to roll with Bowie's space toaster groove, and she let her eyebrows rise then fall at him.

No mistaking her silent objective to connect.

Not in a million years would Evan have thought someone so beautiful, and much younger, could find interest in him. As Patrice's breasts wobbled inside the plunge of her shirt, it was all Evan could do not to bust himself checking them out. Patrice smirked knowingly at Evan as if she *had* busted him, then she pulled her scanner gun out and zapped the UPC bars on the CDs.

"Great pick," she said, pointing down at *Yankee Hotel Foxtrot* and tapping the jewel case with a purple tinted fingernail. It was a slight hue lighter than her shirt, more like a deep lilac, but there was a gleam to the painted nail matching her smile.

Patrice ceased her marginal gyrating and then she swiped Evan's debit card through. He didn't recall ever taking it out of his wallet.

"Thanks, Patrice," Evan replied with raw nerve. Karla's refusal to speak had given him a sudden boldness.

This came with a newly arrived queasiness, and Evan had no interest scarfing down his slapped together roast beef sandwich with Miracle Whip, once he returned to the office. His belly flopped and spun about, just the way it had when he'd first asked Karla out, eighteen years ago.

Patrice's face lit up from Evan's attempt at familiarness as she prompted him. "I look forward to when you come in—"

"Evan."

"Evan. Every other Thursday, we can count on you being here."

"Oh, great, I'm *predictable*," he returned with a muffled laugh. Something quirky ricocheted around his abdomen. Desire? Lust? Shame?

"You and a few other regulars," she joked back, creaking her neck once again. "You have the most eclectic taste, though. I ring you up on purpose just to see what you're picking up. I mean, Wilco, Imelda May, and Herbie Hancock, wow."

"I'm a music dweeb, guilty as charged," Evan said, brazenly peering down Patrice's revealing shirt as she stooped low to grab a bag. Behind her, his receipt was spitting out of its electric roller. Garth-with-a-Crop, aka Neil, caught him and did nothing to hide his simpering chuckle and an upwards rolling of his eyes.

"Music dweebs are my kind of people," Patrice told him, placing a pen down in front of him to sign the sales slip. "And kudos to you on *Going for the One*. I prefer King Crimson and Gentle Giant, but this album gets a bad rap. Maybe because of all the annoying church fugue, but it's still great stuff."

"It's filling the gap in my Yes section," Evan said with a sullied leer he knew advertised his guilt. The same unabashed goofery Chevy Chase laid down in his overcooked flirt game with Nicolette Scorsese, the slender-hipped mall lingerie clerk in *Christmas Vacation*.

Patrice handed Evan his bag which was more rolled up at the top than usual. She'd stapled his receipt copy into the folds.

"Enjoy," she said, offering her hand across the counter. "Good to meet you properly, Evan."

"Same here, Patrice," Evan replied. Her handshake was firm, not petite. It was nowhere near diffident as she normally presented herself, nor was her voice as he left, which now rang with forwardness instead of fragility. He wasn't sure which turned him on more, but he *was* turned on.

"See you when I see you," Patrice said, tittering at Evan. Then she turned and danced away from the register. She forced the curves of her strained jeans like she deserved an audition at a conservatory.

If he hadn't been turned on before, Evan was enthralled now.

The front door bing-bonged behind Evan's departure. Checking his watch a second time, he saw he had nine minutes left of his lunch break. His stomach was settling somewhat, but he was still in no mood to eat.

When he got into his Caliber, Evan tore open the top of the bag, deciding to pop *Going for the One* into the car's CD player. Patrice had raved about it, and this made him smile even harder than he had inside the store. Old guy music from an old guy band, validated by a vibrant youngblood.

Aside from his CDs inside the bag, Evan discovered a folded piece of looseleaf.

"What the...?" he gasped, unfurling it.

I LOVE DAVID BOWIE AND A HAZELNUT WITH NUTMEG AT McCANN COFFEE COMPANY. I GET OFF SHIFT AT 5:30. SEE YOU WHEN I SEE YOU.

Evan smoked not one, but two cigarettes with his car window rolled down on his way back to work. He clocked back in three minutes late.

꿰꿰꿰꿰꿰꿰꿰꿰꿰꿰꿰꿰꿰꿰꿰꿰꿰꿰꿰꿰꿰꿰꿰꿰

When Evan called Karla at home once the end of business came, there was no answer. Part of him hoped she *wouldn't* pick up. She hadn't tried reaching him all day and Evan found himself less offended by it than he'd felt before going to The Chain Effect.

Evan sent Karla a text message after coming up empty on the house phone (one Karla had suggested they disable to save money since everyone used cell phones these days instead of land lines), and again, no response. No answer at her mother's house, who, as a sixty-nine-year-old widow, *did* used a land line in staunch resistance of joining the cellular revolution.

If Karla's mom wasn't picking up, Evan had done far more serious damage than he'd realized. Karla was making a stand.

As he took a whiz in the men's room, Evan tried calling Karla's cell one more time and got her eighth twittery prompt of the day to leave a message. He'd left no less than ten last night, by his estimation. Childish as it was, Evan let the sound of his flushing urinal serve as his latest exchange in her voicemail.

"Fuck it, then," he mumbled on his way out of the office, knowing his next action would likely usher him consequences much worse than a crumbled pack of Camels. If Karla found out, she'd probably *never* come home.

Evan knew he shouldn't, but he worked until 5:20 on purpose and made what would become the worst decision of his life.

This in addition to another smoke on the way to McCann Coffee Company.

𝖩𝖩𝖩𝖩𝖩𝖩𝖩𝖩𝖩𝖩𝖩𝖩𝖩𝖩𝖩𝖩𝖩𝖩𝖩𝖩𝖩𝖩𝖩𝖩𝖩𝖩𝖩𝖩𝖩𝖩𝖩𝖩𝖩𝖩𝖩

McCann Coffee was, Evan decided, a younger person's habitat. At forty-one, he was showing a film of gray amidst his matted-down brown hair. You needed to be up close to find it, but it was the recession from his scalp giving him away — that, plus the beginnings of opaque, puffy bags beneath his eyes, marking him the tired dad he no doubt looked to the much younger patrons half-glancing him.

The low lighting at McCann's contributed to the overall hunkered positioning at the tables and a dominating unruliness dotted with untailored cursing. No better than the repertoires of raw recruit stand-up comics.

Add a gross abundance of caffeine amping the unabashed flagrancy of f-bombs and crotch humor. The only reason Evan excused it all, was because one, he didn't really belong here and two, in his day he could've put half of these kids to shame in the vulgarity department.

Evan was as much a coffee enthusiast as a large percentage of the nation, but he made conventional brand coffee at home every morning since Karla had needled at him it was easier on the budget than hitting Starbucks every day. Evan granted her that point, even if he was growing downright sick of plain-Jane Folgers and Eight O'Clock cannister coffee.

Hawaiian Kona being Evan's favorite and a rare treat, he felt as if he'd been swept into an alternate universe. One with the dazzling cup of house blend Kona he was sipping on across from an equally dazzling young lady who lofted one jean-covered leg across the knee of the other while settling her upright posture. Patrice remained in the same clothes she'd worked in, and it wasn't just Evan — guys *and* girls — dropping their eyes toward her wriggling boobs.

Patrice held her hazelnut with a sprinkle of nutmeg using two hands, circling a ceramic mug bearing the McCann Coffee Company logo in its miniscule blue lettering. Her elevated ankle jittered anxiously.

Like the two of them were on an unstoppable path of sin.

Behind the exultant chatter and ralphing laughter was the googly retro new wave nonsense of The Kooks. In-between, the espresso machine hissed and haaaaed and the blender ground ice. Albeit McCann's blender was such a powerful apparatus its crunching din was wrapped and silenced within a few seconds of starting.

"Noisy place, I know," Patrice projected herself with a weighty pitch, competing with a nearby table of co-eds who roared and smacked on their table like frat house drunks in Celtic-themed bars on never-ending weekends. "It carries its own pulse, though, don't you think?"

"Actually, yeah," Evan confirmed, looking towards the sky-painted ceiling until settling his gaze back on Patrice.

"Why don't you move over next to me?"

Evan nearly blurted the words, "It may be too late to stop this," aloud before stuffing them down and placing his Kona on the opposite side of the ovoid, blue-painted table, then bringing his chair around. His left knee now lurched within inches beneath Patrice's wiggly ankle.

A wolfish whistle knelled from the other end of the room.

"Dad *scores!*" Evan heard amidst the clamor.

"Ignore that jerk," Patrice said, adjusting her posture to face him before patting Evan's thigh. "That prick's name is Clay, and he's still pissed I threw my beer in his face for goosing me during the Fall Out Boy gig at Toccara Theatre last year."

Evan barely heard Patrice, as a warm tingle shot from his midsection up to his chest by the connection of her palm to his leg.

"I remember this joint used to be a secondhand bookstore a lifetime ago," Evan said, composing himself and leaning closer to Patrice so he didn't need to shout.

"And you no doubt supported it religiously like you do *our* store," she returned with a crafty smirk.

"I'm that obvious, huh?" Evan chuckled. "I have boxes of sci-fi and fantasy paperbacks I'll probably never read again, though I hope for a day when I can go back and reread my Piers Anthony and Philip K. Dick books without someone — two little someones in my case — harping on me to watch video games."

"Ah, the original source of *Blade Runner*," Patrice said proficiently. "Dick was a mad genius, and I think androids probably do dream of sheep. Or something, anyway. Something deeper than a 32-bit, open-source Linux Kernal in one of those new HTC Dream phones."

"Wow, I'm impressed," Evan said, sipping on his Kona to stop himself from foolishly adding how hot Patrice had just sounded.

"My older brother, Deron, writes code for Samsung, so I know a little geekspeak. He says they're working on something called Firebase Cloud Messaging which will change the world. That's the extent of what I know in telecommunications. Music-wise, hip hop is still selling better than rock, since we constantly turn around Birdman, Chingy, Scarface, Soulja Boy, Lil Flip, Hurricane Chris, and DJ Khaled. Timbaland and 50 Cent, we always have on back order. None of those rappers ever cross your path?"

"Talib Kweli and Common, sure," Evan answered her smartly with a flash of his coffee-stained teeth. Teeth bombarded by years of java and nicotine, which no whitener could undo. It made Evan feel self-conscious enough to smother them with his lips before resuming. "Those dudes have integrity, but I can't say I'm down with much of today's hip hop. Chuck D and Public Enemy forever."

"You meant Wu-Tang, of course," Patrice joked, immediately growing serious with her anecdote, "When I was kid, some white folks were running in fear of Public Enemy. Many white folks today still only know them, the Beastie Boys, Eminem, and Run-DMC in rap. I hear more white folks today pull Public Enemy as the greatest rap act ever, and that's kind of embarrassing, no offense. For me, it's Nas, the street laureate of the game. MC Lyte if you wanna go old school. D is the fiercest orator I've ever heard, though. Nobody'll ever take that away from him, respect."

"Word," Evan cracked, flashing Patrice a goofy grin he had enough presence to keep lip wrapped.

"Quit while you have me impressed at Kweli, vanilla," Patrice teased, poking Evan's knee with the toe of her shoe. "So, tell me a little about yourself, Evan. All I know about you is there are only two other regulars who drop more coin at The Chain Effect than you. Both vinyl hounds. There's this DJ wannabe who likes to be called 'M,' like in James Bond, right? Then there's this Vietnamese American dude a little younger than you. Nguyen, you know, pronounced like *when*. The guy loves his jazz - Miles Davis, Art Blakey, and such - but he's like you, across the genre board. Except Nguyen's a serious collector. He chases after bootlegs and import pressings, which is how record shops stay alive these days. We love us some Nguyen."

"I would tell you we're on a tight budget at home, but…"

Patrice nearly spit her coffee back out of her mouth by interruption. Once she'd forced it down her throat, she waved her hand up and down in front of her face as if cooling herself or chasing a potential sneeze away.

"That's a laugh," she teased.

"Yeah, yeah, bring it. Look, I'm not going to bellyache over my money issues. You of all people would never believe me."

"Oh, but I do," Patrice said, placing her mug on the table, then squeezing Evan's free arm with both of her hands before releasing just as fast. Women tended to do that, so it often made things difficult for a hard-up guy to detect what was a come-on, and what was just in-the-moment emphatics. "Most people who come into the store are broke ass. They come, they hang, they listen to whatever we're putting out. They pick up albums, pretend they're considering buying them, then put them back. All a pose. Repeat cycle for a half hour or more, then they leave. Please, *I'm* no different. I barely make my rent and utilities. But then, I have a generous employee discount."

"We all have our vices," Evan noted. "My problem is I have to hide mine from my wife."

"Hmm. You're hitched, huh? How's that working for you, since you're here hanging with a younger woman of color instead of where you *should* be?"

The insinuation behind Patrice's probing gave Evan a flutter of the wrong kind. He would've chastised himself for mentioning he was married, but married was married, and accordingly, he knew what he was doing was not only improper, but dicey.

"We had a fight, if I'm going keep to sounding like a cliché," Evan quipped, trying to play it cool and sipping on his Kona to keep his piling nerves in check. "Karla and I have been together almost half our lives. We have two boys, twins. Jared and Isaac. She's a bit hardline at times, like I should condemn her. She's the conscience in our marriage, I'm man enough to say it. She's a pain in my ass, though I'm far more of one to her. I'm afraid to total up the money I've pissed away on CDs this year alone."

"And let me guess, it's been months since she's put out."

"Close to an entire year," Evan let slip, feeling awful for it, but at the same time, knowing it was going to be said. Thus, he added, "No excuses, no apologies for the out-of-nowhere shutting of the pipes. Just the shutting part."

"Damn," Patrice said, counterfeiting a look of surprise. Evan detected the fake and still let it fly, knowing he'd put himself on a course of no return. All he could wonder at this point was if Patrice wore a thong or regular panties. Lavender, at that.

"Patrice," Evan next said in an even tone, unshaken by Patrice's assertion. If anything, her sexual bravado gave Evan a glimmer of hope, and his slacks were strained with craving. There was a deep tickle inside his balls, desperate for satiation.

Audaciousness sealing his fate, Evan sat his coffee down and placed his free hand on top of Patrice's upright knee. "We don't know each other very well, but there's something about you I like. What I say next might be considered too forward, but..." He paused.

"Go for it," Patrice interjected, inhaling, then spreading a smile of consent. She left Evan's hand on her knee as if it belonged there.

"I admit I have a spending problem and I also get strung out at times when I can't have a cigarette. I've been trying like to hell to quit altogether. *Everyone* who smokes goes through this awful withdrawal shit, right? I know my wife's heart is in the right place, but at the same time, last night I said something I shouldn't have. She'd crossed the line first, though. I only smoke a few times a week, usually discreetly, but last night after Karla left with our boys, I attacked a fresh pack like most people would an all-you-can-eat sushi bar. Today I haven't exactly been strict on myself, as well. Is that bad?"

"No worse than being good to yourself in our store," Patrice said with that calming grin Evan was growing fonder of every time he saw it.

"To my knowledge there's no such thing as Record Store Anonymous."

Patrice's eyes blossomed and she let loose a giggle-cackle that sounded like Betty Rubble on a good toot. "I'd be out of a job if there was such a thing!"

Another leering whistle pierced through the racket. This time, Patrice abruptly rose from her seat, dumping Evan's hand back into his lap. Her composure seeped away and what Evan saw now was an unexpected severe expression. One daring anyone to trifle with her.

"Get a life, douchebag!" she screamed and flipped the offending party off.

From his seated position, Evan couldn't tell who Patrice was throwing down at, not until he'd heard said offending party flout her, "Go fuck yourself, ni—"

"Say it!" Patrice roared back, launching at the guy. Bring Me the Horizon's rambunctious "It Never Ends" turned miniscule overhead. "Say it, you racist piece of shit! Oh, I *dare* you, motherfucker!"

It wasn't scary enough Patrice had brought the roof down with her voice. She'd closed in on the guy, discernable to Evan for only a flash. He was a beanpole, greasy-haired hick type, likely in Patrice's and most everyone else at McCann Coffee's age bracket. His jeans were filthier than the oily strands dangling beneath his ears. Evan could have sworn the guy was wearing one of those old *Austin 3:16* tees, one Evan presumed had been baptized by as many beers as pro wrestling icon "Stone Cold" Steve Austin himself did taunting opponents on national television inside the squared circle.

Patrice may not have had the flip bigot set up with his chin draped across her shoulder for one of Austin's patented 'stunners,' but as Evan rose out of his seat, he could see she had the guy's right wrist pinned to his table. Her other hand was spread across the underweight xenophone's throat. Her thumb and fourth fingers were burrowed into either side of his jaw.

He was gagging ferociously, his face flushing pink in a hurry. His eyes watered as he hocked and forced himself to breathe. Patrice's strength was such that he couldn't budge his trapped hand.

Only when he had enough presence of mind to use his free hand did Patrice let go to avoid his sloppy, half-dazed swing.

"I'll gut you if I ever see you again, white trash," she hissed into his face, pointing her nails at the bloody hollows she'd left beneath his ears.

"You need to leave, Patrice," a new voice entered the scene, belonging to a husky Hispanic woman everyone who frequented McCann Coffee lovingly referred to as "Tia Livia." As in everyone's take-no-shit but lovable honorary aunt, Livia Sanchez, manager of an Irish-named coffeehouse.

"What?! This waste of sperm was saying—" Patrice objected, though turning her juice down.

"I heard it all and he's no longer welcome here," Tia Livia said with enough authority to quash any potential challenge from the guy, who was rubbing both sides of his jaw with a bitter if checked-down leer at Patrice. "I don't care who's right or who's wrong in this matter. This is my shift, my watch, and I'm putting a stop to this before this argument turns into a race riot. Come back another day, girl. Let the sun fall on this one as it should."

"Drink up, babe," Patrice said to Evan with a fire in her eyes, purposefully dipping her stance to give Evan as much of a gawk at her joggling chest as he wanted. Like she knew he was interested. "We're out. I have a one-bedroom job less than a mile from here. I'm in the mood for some frozen pizza, *Aladdin Sane* and more than one shot of tequila. I'll be damned if I'm doing it alone."

Evan wasn't sure what was making him dizzier, the successive hits of Pueblo Viejo blanco Patrice had pushed at him rapid-fire, or the countless albums passing through his hands within the first hour he'd been at her place. He'd already felt caught in a whirlwind after her roughhouse dealings at McCann Coffee. Frightened to some extent. Arousal coming with each successive minute at her place.

No surprise, Patrice had all of David Bowie's records including a handful of vinyl bootlegs from his mid-Seventies *Plastic Soul* tours.

"I like you," she said, "but I'm not spinning those for anybody." Afterwards, she placed a tiny peck on Evan's cheek before vanishing to the open-view kitchen to throw in a frozen pizza.

The fly-by kiss gave Evan the shivers after first recoiling from her advance. Partly because Evan knew what was coming, especially after checking his cell phone to find no incoming calls or texts.

Patrice's collection ranged from Prince to Wynton Marsalis to The Smiths to Stereolab to PJ Harvey to Ministry to The Jam plus all genres in between. Evan was especially impressed to see the Subhumans, Kraftwerk, and Can represented. It was like he'd met a younger female version of himself.

"You know, Patrice, I'm fascinated someone your age is this much into older artists," he said, more to simmer his bundling tension.

"Alright, funny man," Patrice fired back, but with none of the rancor she'd exhibited in the coffeehouse. She sounded soft, now. Relaxed. Cute, even. Like she usually did at The Chain Effect. "Not too many guys *your* age is pulling Wilco, Vampire Weekend, and Bell X1 off the shelves. You go for the young *with* the old."

"Touché," Evan said in appreciation of her generation gap jab. Instead of making him feel awkward, it gave him an opposite reaction. "What, no mini shrine to Bowie around here? Not a Ziggy poster to be found on the premises. And you call yourself a *fan*?"

"I used to have a vintage subway poster with the *Scary Monsters* cover art on it," Patrice responded with more seriousness than Evan anticipated. "Until Deron, that shithead, came home stoned one night, yanked it down from my room and set it on fire in a trash barrel. 'We don't listen to that cracker crap,' he told me as he torched that poster, the asshole. If enlightened white people like you can come up to the counter with Fela Kuti, Bobatunde Olatunji, and Jurassic 5, *I* can be a David Bowie fan."

"Man, you have an incredible memory, and I guess your brother's never seen the color of Bowie's second wife."

Patrice covered her mouth as she giggled. "Deron's a fuck-up sometimes, but he's smarter than hell and I love him, even if the poster's still a sore subject with me. Cost me fifty bucks to have it shipped from France, man. Suffice it to say, I don't have that kind of cash these days, as if you can't tell by the *Better Homes and Gardens* décor of my place."

She hadn't been kidding; the single bedroom in Patrice's apartment was a short, empty walk at the end of a short, empty corridor. Her cramped bathroom was practical, at least for a single girl. She'd thrown mock faboo into her presentation by opening her tiny medicine cabinet storing all of two shelves and a mere bottle of ibuprofen occupying one of them. "The pharmacy's down a block if you need more than that," she'd joked.

Her kitchen and dining room combined for the apartment's most spacious area and neither had much beyond the basics. Her rickety oval dinner table with its unsound metal legs was big enough to handle four customers, though Patrice only had two chairs with cheap bamboo backrests to accompany it. Both had their foam inserts belching out from split open seat cushions, looking like they'd been around when David Bowie had released the *Low* album in 1977.

Patrice's sofa and loveseat were equally antediluvian. Evan was sunken into the ratty loveseat with its hideous maroon shag upholstery and a hundred disengaged lint balls, ripe for picking. It also smelled of various things, ranging from spilled fingernail polish remover to Cheetos to weed. Other than that, Patrice had a small TV with a DVD player mounted atop the console, a Goodwill-discounted coffee table with a strained pressboard top about ready to splinter, plus her ceiling-high media shelf stocked full of CDs, DVDs, and 33-rpm records.

On the flipside, Patrice did have a stellar Pioneer turntable considered top-of-the-line for 1986 and still cranking beauteously, plus a Sony five-disc CD player. Both were planted upon a two-tiered rolling entertainment cart with a pull-open cabinet. More videos and albums were stored inside. Waist-high floor speakers guarded both sides of the cart. Evan pitied Patrice's neighbors, but not too much. He'd been momentarily startled by her aggression at McCann Coffee earlier. Now he was in awe.

Patrice had thrown on rasta punk and reggae legends Bad Brains and their blistering *Rock for Light* album, and she danced, thrashed, pogoed, and spun with graceful, thump-reduced gyrations on the faster cuts, the raging anarchy serving as her backdrop. Then she slow-rolled her moves on the gradual, calmer reggae cuts like "Rally 'Round Jah Throne," "The Meek Shall Inherit the Earth," and "I and I Survive." Afterwards, Patrice spun half of Fiona Apple's *When the Pawn* while matching Evan three rounds of clear tequila in the short time span.

Then the main attraction, a perfectly crisped Red Baron sausage pizza accompanied by David Bowie's *Aladdin Sane*.

"The pizza's as Gucci as my crib," Patrice kidded between album changes and handing Evan a paper plate with two hot pieces on it. She'd also refilled his shot glass. "Four pies for ten bucks at Carpenter's Corner, no better deal in town. Except maybe the tequila, inexpensive and you can taste the mint and agave before the white pepper. Pueblo Viejo's my go-to. Cheers."

Evan started swooning within the first few strokes of "Watch That Man," accompanied by his fifth shot of Pueblo Viejo and a bite of the thin, crispy pizza. Patrice was already on shot number seven before she began pulling straight from the bottle. Patrice appeared to be a drinking pro, while the booze was beginning to take its toll on Evan.

She slowly grooved her waist in time with "Drive-In Saturday," rolling it like a trophy belly dancer, then closing her eyes and opening them with transitory glances at Evan. When the sassy and sleazy "Cracked Actor" arrived, she'd placed the tequila bottle between Evan's legs and snickered, singing along with Bowie, "Smack baby, smack, is that all you feel?"

Patrice turned her rear towards Evan and gave each cheek a whack before elevating on one foot and pirouetting in the middle of her close-quartered living room. She was graceful in her moves, even with all she'd consumed, though she'd missed clipping her ankle on the cheap coffee table by mere inches.

"Were you into ballet in another life?" Evan sloshed, the alcohol doing a number on him. It had been nearly as long since he'd been laid, as drinking so recklessly.

"Nah, my parents couldn't afford to send me to classes, not even at the YMCA where every poor sucker sends their kids for sports and shit, but I do like to dance."

"I guess Bowie just brings it out of you," Evan said, pulling the tequila to his lips, pausing a moment to consider how another hit might send him full tilt. To himself, he whispered while snatching another slug, despite, "Screw it, anything goes from this point forward."

"You know, the Spiders lineup totally rules," Patrice opined about David Bowie's early years, "but there are so many tasteless jerkoffs who rag on the Brian Eno years. I'm only a girl in a record store old enough to be the man's granddaughter, but in my humble opinion, Eno and Bowie made a lot of magic together."

The room was starting to spin so quickly Evan hadn't noticed Patrice was straddling him in the raunchy loveseat as she lowered her groin towards the bottle back between his legs, working the edge of the nozzle perversely through her stiff jeans. As if by decree of the rock gods, "The Jean Genie" strutted into action from the stereo as Patrice loosened the snap of her denim. Then she grabbed Evan's right hand and pinched his fingers onto her zipper.

For a second Evan's hand trembled, knowing he was doing far worse to his marriage than sneaking smokes and CDs behind Karla's back.

"Go ahead, baby," Patrice murmured.

Loud as the music was, Evan heard nothing else for a long time.

Patrice kissed him ravenously, her agave-coated tongue darting all over his. Evan was amateurish by comparison, considering it had been years since Karla had frenched him. He tasted a wicked brew of sausage, tomato sauce, and the mint Patrice had alluded to. It delighted him as much the cool air and warm hand greeting his freed, flappity penis.

Evan felt something transfer between their mouths, something leafy from what he could tell in the instant it passed from Patrice's mouth to his. It barely touched Evan's tongue, which hungrily sought Patrice's in response to her flickering teases. By then, the salvia leaf had already slid down his throat.

Then came the sound of a twinkling, candelabra-hinted piano intro to Bowie's "Lady Grinning Soul," painting an air of sophistication and peril as Bowie swooned about clothes being strewn and not being afraid of the room before divvying his ominous lyrical warning, "She'll be your living end."

Unclothed and on his back, a broil swam throughout Evan's body. Evan's world went pitch black as he was engulfed by Patrice, who seized his shudder inside of her, before whispering, "Come on vanilla, I want your cream."

ппппппппппппппппппппппппппппп

Evan found himself staring into oblivion, as naked as he'd ever been, before passing out.

Patrice was nowhere to be found, yet Evan's connection to her was still evident, with the repetitive riffs of David Bowie's "Rebel Rebel" echoing all around him. One of Bowie's most recognizable hits. Evan was hearing the guitar licks only, no vocals from the man who was no longer vamping his alter ego Ziggy Stardust by the time "Rebel Rebel" and the *Diamond Dogs* album came out.

"Hot tramp, I love you so," Evan found himself glubbing into the inky ether. His voice sounded not only slurred, but slowed altogether, reminiscent of playing his Kiss and Alice Cooper 45-vinyl singles on the turntable at a slower 33-rpm speed as a kid. Hilarious tonal shenanigans he'd repeated for his own sons, who'd laughed themselves silly when Evan had slowed down The Turtles' already trippy love ditty, "You Showed Me" for them.

This is what Evan sounded like right now as he sought out Patrice with a blurry hand. It was one of those fractal image effects he'd seen in plenty of action and drug drama flicks, where the appendage seemed to leave splintering sections of itself in transition, the segments adjoining upon stoppage.

With the sound of buzzsaw guitars growing thunderous, an entire urban cityscape sprawled all around Evan, who pushed himself to stand on newly laid road. He saw the pavement, but didn't feel it, like he'd grown numb standing there, bare-assed in witness of an encompassing erection of skyscrapers, rowhomes, museums, delicatessens and a manna of neon advertising. The sky around the risen metropolis was glassy, shimmering. Like Evan had been plugged inside a city-in-a-bottle.

"You've gotta be kidding me," he muttered, no longer sounding loopy. His voice was becoming as concrete as the manifesting conurbation.

As real as the sudden nip upon his bare right ankle.

"Ow! What the—" Evan snapped as he leaned to the side and spotted a natty rat thrice the usual size. About the size of a standard tabby cat. It looked up at Evan with an imploring gaze from its rose-pink, flushed eyes and only then did he see the trail of guts and intestines barely clinging to the rest of the squeaking carcass.

Chewing on the rat itself was an impossibly huge insect, not one of those scorpion flies or dobsonflies Evan had seen on Animal Planet some weekend ago with Karla curled on the sofa with him, her feet planted into his lap. So soon had their toned-down affections become trivial.

A gnat, hundreds of times larger than its proper size in the grand scheme of nature (something even the late, ballsy eco-warrior Steve Irwin might've shriveled from), sunk its hideous incisors into the rat, which shrieked its final death throes up at Evan before dropping its head to the concrete.

"Jesus!" Evan fizzled, leaping away as the monster gnat gobbled on the rat's remains with nauseating slurps, chasing away "Rebel Rebel's" back-and-forth sashay.

For whatever reason, Evan felt a need to cup his hands around his genitals, even if this—wherever the hell it was—city was devoid of other humans. As empty as certain violence-chewed pockets of Manhattan-turned-into-a-prison in *Escape from New York.* The only sense of direction Evan could detect was a signpost with one-way marked 17th Street, its cross-section denoted, crazily enough, "Love-Me Avenue."

"Patrice?" Evan blurted, circling in place, and still finding nobody else before he released his privates. They'd felt sweaty and sticky, even inside this trapped illusion.

It *was* an illusion, wasn't it?

"Where'd you go, Patrice, and where the hell am I?"

As if in answer, a beam of light rendered ineffective fluorescent ads for Coca-Cola, Camel cigarettes, a rapid moving video pitch for *Kung-Fu Panda,* Jared and Isaac's current favorite movie, and Viagra pills. The ray, as blinding and outlandish as those nasty spirits of Native vengeance in *Poltergeist,* overtook them all, spotlighting the skyscraper nearest Evan with intention. The marble marquee above the stilled revolving doors announced the building's name as TEMPERENCE.

The refraction of the tinted windows seared Evan's vision for a split second as he felt another bite into his ankle.

The same spot where the rat tagged him and where Evan had failed to notice, he'd bled.

In its place was a rotted human skeleton, its ribcage slung with a brownish muck looking like flushed turds. Eye sockets hollowed yet streaming with viscous liquids pouring down into its mucky jawline. What would've been a brown, bushy mustache upon skin had somehow remained upon bone, as did a waggly goatee. Absurd to be sure, Evan had a similar image sprawled across album covers in his collection covering genres ranging from heavy metal to country to folk-styled jam bands.

"Every dog has its day," the skeleton-thing squelched at Evan like it was drowning. It seized Evan with its bone-

exposed fingers, elongated nails from each digit sinking into Evan's left thigh, tearing into it, and yielding squirts of blood feeling all too real to Evan. Hot, branding, painful, and coming with the seeping indictment, *"Infidelity ushers your final hour. A succubus shall be your living end."*

As he fell to the pavement, Evan saw what hadn't been there before, scores of rotting bodies, many of them piled in front of the Temperence Building.

Suuuuuccuuuuubuuuuus, the skeleton-thing echoed as the sunlight dimmed and the faux city fell into a despairing dusk.

The neon ads reasserted themselves, this time flashing the word CHEATER at Evan. It was written in the same curly-cue swirl where Coca-Cola would usually be. It was there on the *Kung-Fu Panda* ad, where Po-Ping, the titular martial arts bear chop-sockeyed his way through a granite-styled title card, not for the movie, but an unmade flick, CHEATER. It exploded and reformed, over and over, as Po-Ping pummeled it on repeat.

Evan hollered in both anger and fear to see the Viagra ad taunting him further in blinking sequences, *CAUGHT IN A RUT WHEN YOU'RE CROTCH-HUNTING AWAY FROM HOME? POP A VIAGRA AND BE KING OF THE JUNGLE ONCE AGAIN.*

A fissure slashed through what little of the sky remained from sight as the buildings began listing toward the center of his view in a combined collapse straight down on him.

A glowing pair of red eyes glared down at Evan before the edifices crushed him. Judgmental, condemnatory eyes.

Repent now, adulterer, Evan heard before the sight of disgusting sinew and cavity-chewed teeth bore down on him.

ⁿⁿⁿⁿⁿⁿⁿⁿⁿⁿⁿⁿⁿⁿⁿⁿⁿⁿⁿⁿⁿⁿⁿⁿⁿⁿⁿⁿⁿⁿⁿ

"Wake up, honey," was what Evan heard next. "You were seriously tripping."

"Patrice?" Evan blubbered, feeling tears spill from his eyes and a throbbing inside of his right ankle where he'd been attacked. His inner thigh on the same leg felt prickly, like he'd fucked Patrice inside a sumac patch instead of her apartment.

He was still lying on his back. Still naked. Still sticky between his legs, sticky beneath his back and butt. Sticky beneath the backs of his arms and legs. Stickiest, of all things, at the bottom of his right leg.

"Yeah, baby," she answered, placing a cooling sable hand down his right cheek. Her thumb wiped away the salty residue.

Unlike Evan, Patrice was clothed. This time in a tight pair of gray leggings and a David Bowie shirt representing the cover for *The Man Who Sold the World*.

"What'd you give me, Christ?"

"A little Sally-D," she said, pulling her hand away. She was straddled across Evan's lap.

For some reason now, he couldn't feel his right ankle, only a residual aching. As if the skeletal monstrosity in the hallucination had sent him back to consciousness with something to remember it by.

"Maria Pastora," Patrice went on. "A little hit of Mexican salvia, Evan. Tia Livia at the coffeehouse gets it on the down low all the time. Why do you think so many young people go there, huh? We call her our 'Auntie' since she has mad hookups. Shrooms, Molly, microdots, skag, whatever you want, she can get it. Except for that Russian Krokodil morphine shit. Fine by me, since even I have my limits."

"What the hell, Patrice?" Evan protested. "Why?"

"Oh, baby, chill out," she said. "You were having a little problem getting it up at first, but once you were flying high on the Magic Mint, that did the ticket. I think it's the buried fear of getting caught which spikes the adrenal glands even when blocking the erection for a moment, but you filled me the hell *up*, vanilla. Don't worry, I take Femodette along with my recs, so you won't get me pregnant."

"My wife," Evan blathered, feeling, for the first time, actual shame.

"She doesn't matter anymore," Patrice said with such calm it alarmed Evan. Even more so sprawled out with her locking his midsection in place. He tried moving his arms and legs, yet he couldn't right now. "She's been blowing up your phone since you passed out, though. I guess the fight's over."

"Oh, my God," Evan grunted, lifting both of his arms, and realizing the surface beneath them peeled away and made a crinkly cadence, like —

"The first text says she's sorry for what she called you, isn't that sweet?" Patrice went on, planting her hands upon Evan's bare chest with such force it was like a car had rolled on top of him. The air went out of his lungs, begging for respite from his nostrils and esophagus, both tightening with Patrice's deep compression. "She says your boys miss you and so does she. Aww, I almost feel bad about this. The next text, she's sounding a little worried. The last one, well, she's in a complete panic now. She's called twenty times, it seems."

"I—I gotta go," Evan squeezed out, his head crashing over and over from the decrease in oxygen. It was then, with his rising delirium and shortness of breath, with the fictile rumpling beneath his thrashing legs and arms, he realized he was lying on the floor of Patrice's apartment.

Not on thin carpet.

On a rolled-out tarp.

"Nuh uh, baby," Patrice told him, peering down into his face, the tip of her nose grazing his. Her breath reeked worse than alcohol and cheap pizza, like she'd sucked on a slab of raw meat while he'd been out. Worse, her glaring eyes dilated then flushed with blood, submerging the pupils before leaking cerise flows down her cheeks. "You're not going anywhere. You're mine now."

"What the fuck?!?" Evan exclaimed to see a foot whisk into his view. Recently sliced with gory gristle and rubbery skin tissue flapping about. Bone shards jutting from the stump. Like one of those silly prop Halloween gimmicks, only the severed foot was real.

That was when it dawned on Evan the pain lighting up again was from an ankle no longer there.

"Not a bad come," Patrice whispered. waggling the gummy musculature of Evan's shorn foot above his face. Rivulets of his own blood dotted his cheeks and his lips. "Acceptable under the circumstances, though it's more about the cutting than the fucking with me, Evan, if you want the truth."

Patrice placed Evan's sopping red ankle on his chest gently, with such care and precision it took his concentration away from the upraised black handled serrated bone saw in her right hand. The jagged teeth already glistening with blood.

"Karla, I'm so—"

Evan's screams as Patrice kissed him goodbye turned into nauseating gurgling with each pass of the saw.

Author's Note

Horror has been in my blood nearly all my life, starting with those bittersweet late-night Saturdays in competition with my stepsister and stepbrother watching the classic Universal monster mashes and 1950s atomic B movies on *Ghost Host*, Baltimore's answer to Dr. Dementia, Zacherley, The Cool Ghoul and the

original Svengoolie, Jerry G. Bishop. Jiffy-Pop, Suburban Almond Smash, rabbit ear antennae. You had to have been there. Scooby-Doo came before that, my generation's training wheels to riding hard and riding free in the horror realm.

In November of 1979 I received my first jolt as a future horror freak, and it's been a love affair ever since. I'll never forget it and neither do my peers, since it's become Gen X canon. I'm talking about the CBS prime-time miniseries adaptation of Stephen King's *Salem's Lot.*

Specifically, that terrifying pipsqueak vampire Danny Glick, still in his pajamas floating and scratching upon the window for his little buddy Mark Petrie to let him inside his bedroom. Forty-five years later as of this writing, it's still a goddamned creepy sequence. I thought of it often while writing the stories for *Behind the Shadows.*

It was that frightening scene which had turned me not only into a horror freak, but a lifetime Stephen King acolyte as well. I found myself itching to read the source behind such terror, yet I had to wait until age twelve when my grandfather deemed me old enough to be diving into more adult-oriented novels instead of Laura Ingalls Wilder's *Little House of the Prairie* and Betsy Byers stories I'd been weaned on along with a steady diet of comic books. Cussing, gore, sex. I saw his point right off-the-bat, but I wanted all I could get of it.

Grandpop was more of a pulp fiction fan who adored the mercenary mayhem of Casca, Mack Bolan, and The Executioner, yet he spotted me examining paperback copies of King's works on one of our shopping outings. I must have had that pathetic, longing look in my eyes most acquisitive tweens do, because we came out of a long-gone department store in Essex, Maryland called Kresge's with a bag of King's books. I'd crossed into a magnificent monster-filled world with *Salem's Lot, Cujo, Night Shift, Firestarter, Carrie* and the book which blew me away so much it issued me my marching orders to write: *The Shining*.

Enough of the nostalgia stuff.

I began penning the stories for *Behind the Shadows* immediately after the acceptance of my previous novel, *Revolution Calling* from Raw Earth Ink last year. Writing that deeply personal story and connecting with the metal and horror loving teen I was during the 1980s rekindled a spark which had faded some while I was covering local news and NHL hockey games. This before the heavy music and horror film industries welcomed me in, where I reviewed domestic and international media, shot live concert photography, and interviewed countless personalities. It was an incredible side career I've never taken for granted. They have their place driving me to this point in *Behind the Shadows*.

These tales of terror you've just read come from binges of Godzilla films, the original *Twilight Zone, Shameless, Masters of Horror, The X-Files,* EC and *Haunted Horror* Comics, *Heavy Metal* illustrated fantasy magazine, plus Garth Ennis and Steve Dillon's *Preacher,* the gold standard of sardonic horror punk. They were crafted with the daunting atmospherics of John Carpenter, Jerry Goldsmith, Goblin, Krzysztof Komeda, Junkie XL, Lalo Schifrin and Pino Dinaggio film scores, along with albums by Voivod and Iron Maiden. Liquid Metal, 1stWave, and Smokey's Soul Town filled the gaps while behind the wheel plugged into Sirius XM.

I found kindred spirits in films like *Hereditary, A Quiet Place, Tokyo Zombie, The Last Voyage of the Demeter, Lust/Caution, The Sadness, Audition, Tusk* and *Midsommar,* the latter two leaving their scars upon me in the same fashion as *Make Them Die Slowly* way back in the day. Cheers to unstoppable renaissance man Nicolas Cage for *Mandy, Willy's Wonderland,* and *Renfield.* All these lunatic flicks gave me verve as I wrote *Behind the Shadows.*

I could list an easy hundred writers who have inspired me, more than a handful being voices who helped mold these stories. Several of you I consider friends and I thank you for sharing your

wisdom and camaraderie. You know who you are, brothers and sisters, however I must give my deepest thanks to Mike, Dayton, Chris, Billy, John, Josh, Sheila, Jack, and Joshua. Bless you for your generosity. Thanks to the immeasurable Matt Slay for his outrageously savage cover art. I conjured a concept along the lines of *The Howling* and *Wolverine,* Volume 1, Issue 50, bringing something new and unsettling to the theme. I wanted a statement made right off-the-bat, and to coin a corny if befitting pun, Matt *slayed* it.

To my wife, TJ, I love you. Everyone says it when they see us together; we make sense, we belong together. My writing has been not a fountain but a geyser since we got together. I've written like a madman this past year and you're the catalyst. Thank you for becoming my wife last fall, for believing in me and kicking my ass when I say I suck or I should just give up. I just might have without you.

To you, dear readers, thank you for reading *Behind the Shadows,* and anything else preceding it with my name affixed. Writing horror is what I've wanted to do for so *very* long. Just ask my mother, family, and my oldest friends. It happened guys, *finally.*

Yeah. I really was a comic book retail clerk once and that day of the *Superman* 75 reprints really did happen. Before the meteor of doom struck, of course. I experienced some of the other scenarios in these stories, but the biggest takeaway is my bibles in

EC, *Creepshow,* Rod Serling, Bram Stoker, and baseball called to me the loudest as I wrote, often at fever pitch.

I hope I have been able to bring something to the table in a genre carrying the paradox of demanding both the best and the worst of its scribes. Keeping things in context, of course.

Behind the Shadows has been the most gratifying project I've ever done and I'm nowhere near finished with the mission.

Mark Petrie, don't you *dare* open that window!

~Ray Van Horn, Jr.

About the Author

RAY VAN HORN, JR. is the author of *Behind the Shadows, Revolution Calling,* and *Coming of Rage.* Ray spent sixteen years covering music and film for outlets such as Blabbermouth, *AMP, Pit,* Dee Snider's House of Hair, *Music Dish, DVD Review,* Horror News.net, *Fangoria Musick, Hails & Horns, Metal Maniacs, Noisecreep* and many others.

Ray was an NHL game analyst for *The Hockey Nut.* His work has appeared in *Rue Morgue, Eternal Haunted Summer, Punk Noir, Atomic Flyswatter, Horror Tree, Cyber Age Adventures, Flash in a Flash, The Rubbertop Review, Story Bytes, Quantum Muse* and *New Noise,* plus the anthologies *Horror A-Z: X, Axes of Evil* and *Axes of Evil II.*